MARINER TWENTY

Published by Novel Novella Publishing
East Sussex, United Kingdom

ISBN 978-1-84396-681-4

Also available as a Kindle ebook
978-1-84396-633-3

This is a work of fiction. Any resemblance
between the characters and situations depicted and
those in real life is purely coincidental.

Reviews

When zillionaire entrepreneur Roger Haines acquired a piece of land that had a crystal cavern, it quickly became the essential factor in cementing the success of the Mariner Twenty Project; the first human mission to Mars. The task is to develop the first base for an eventual human colony. Six astronauts of various backgrounds and specialties carry on the mission as best as they can according to plan but the red planet has surprises waiting to be discovered.

Mariner Twenty is a contemporary sci-fi novel by G.D. Harrison. No doubt inspired by NASA's missions to Mars, Mariner Twenty is a realistic glimpse of the future missions that could be done involving the red planet. As we follow the Perseverance rover that continues to make substantial progress on the surface of Mars, this is quite a read from G.D. Harrison"

Reviewed by Lit Amri for *Readers' Favorite*

Splitting between action on Mars as the crew attempt to set up the first human colony, reflections by Haines and realistic press conferences where the world's media gather to learn as much as they can about this ground breaking mission, the reader sees all sides of the Mariner Twenty project. Right down to the previously mentioned press conference, this story has a very realistic feel about it. There are moments of tension and the plot slowly develops a sci-fi edge as a select group at Mission Control must make a decision that could decide the future of the human race.

I found that *Mariner Twenty* was an easy to read and well-constructed story that can be enjoyed in one sitting with an ending that allows an opportunity to consider human behaviour."
Reviewed by LoveReading Ambassador

MARINER TWENTY

G D Harrison

NOVEL NOVELLA PUBLISHING

Contents

CHAPTER ONE
The Five Million Dollar Ram

Carlos Da Silva was a rich man; a very rich man. He also had a limp, which he thought was worth the inconvenience. Having been the owner of his own sheep farm in Central America, he was used to small injuries and small inconveniences, but his limp was the result of a fortunate fall into a hidden cave on his land that occurred over a decade ago. If he hadn't spent several hours looking for a lost ram, then he wouldn't have fallen through some unstable ground and into a hidden underworld that had given him his fortune. For, if he hadn't fallen through the surface, he wouldn't have met the zillionaire Roger Haines, who was an entrepreneur of epic proportions.

The limp was ultimately worth $5,000,000 to Carlos but this wasn't an industrial injury payment from an insurance policy. This is what Roger Haines paid Carlos for his land, but that was small change to Roger, for his purchase was probably worth a million times that amount, and therefore the farmland that Carlos eventually sold to Roger for that incredible amount, was a good deal for both men.

The cavern that Carlos fell into was a true crystal maze and held numerous perfectly formed glinting glass forms, one of which had broken off from its moorings when Carlos had crashed into the virgin land beneath him. The small piece of crystal was about three centimetres long and a centimetre wide, with four perfectly equal triangular-shaped angles at the end, which formed a point at each terminus. Carlos kept it as a souvenir, and having eventually clambered out of his temporary prison, he would show his prize to a very few selected friends and family.

Somehow Roger Haines became aware of Carlos Da Silva and his souvenir, and so intrigued was he that he travelled in person to try and locate both Carlos and his find. Eventually the two men met by chance in a local bar, although Roger's team had done an extraordinary amount of searching to turn chance into probability.

The two individuals looked a strange sight. The American, Roger Haines, was a tall man who was dressed in a casual manner, with a linen beige jacket and plain grey tee shirt atop a pair of nicely fitting blue denim jeans. A pair of hiking sandals finished the image. The whole vision was one of an expensive casually dressed man in his late thirties, with a tanned complexion setting off perfectly his mid blond hair and blue eyes.

By contrast, Carlos was a good twenty centimetres shorter, hunched slightly with a body tilt that favoured his non-limping side. He was naturally tanned with a heavily ridged face that was born from a lifetime of working outside in the Central American sunshine. His age had to be guessed at – sixty, maybe seventy. Dark brown eyes and matching hair, that hadn't been combed in weeks, completed his collection of physical attributes. His dress was equally casual but hadn't been achieved by design; his was working casual with a dusty film covering his red checked shirt and ill-fitting blue jeans. A pair of old brown working boots rooted him to the floor.

Roger Haines positioned himself in an appropriate zone at the bar counter and eventually engineered a conversation to persuade Carlos to show him the small crystal. At first Carlos was reluctant to increase his circle of fellow crystal enthusiasts, but so persuasive was the entrepreneur that Carlos eventually admitted defeat and retrieved the item from a front pocket of his jeans. He didn't question how Roger Haines knew who he was, or that he had a crystal, but that was the side effect of too many beers on a sunny afternoon.

The crystal was wrapped in a small piece of old sack cloth. As Carlos unwrapped it the sunlight beamed through the window of the bar and bounced through the crystal from various different angles. To the non-scientific members of the bar (which was all of them apart from Roger Haines), it was just a piece of crystal that provided a pretty light show, but this crystal held special properties.

As Carlos held the crystal up in his right hand, and the light had a clear line of sight through it, the direction of the beam shone a corresponding show onto the plain wall in front of them. The expected array of rainbow colours wasn't on display; there were just two bands of a blueish mauve hue that fell equidistant from a central black line. Roger Haines tried to hide his glee at the vision which was displayed in front of him. He had found the most valuable product in the world.

Carlos, whilst proud of his souvenir, was also wary of any unwanted advances beyond a casual chat over a beer or two. But there was something about Roger's demeanour that made the two men warm to each other, and therefore it wasn't too much of a hardship for Carlos to agree to the natural request that Roger put to him:

"Would you consider showing me where you found this?" he said, in his perfectly educated West Coast accent.

"Maybe," responded Carlos, in a classic broken English Hispanic tone, whilst gesticulating that his beer glass was empty. Roger Haines took the hint and ordered a pair of beers for the now negotiating couple. Carlos continued:

"I can show you the cavern but not where it is. We blindfold, yes?"

This put Roger Haines in a difficult position. As a multi-billionaire his life was extremely valuable to any would-be thief or kidnapper, and even though his counterpart might not have realised who exactly he was speaking to, Roger always had to be on his guard. He had entered the bar alone but he also had a couple of support guys sitting in an off-road Jeep outside. He also had a location chip embedded in his back. He was willing to take the risk for the prize on offer.

"Okay!" he said, raising his glass to clink with the glass of his new best friend.

"We drink this. We then go, yes?" concluded Carlos.

Roger smiled in agreement and the two tilted their heads back in unison to conclude the first part of their meeting.

Carlos too had an entourage with him and as he placed his empty glass on the counter, two of his brothers approached the bar.

"Puedes conseguir un saco de la furgoneta?" asked Carlos.

This was not aimed at Roger, but having lived on the West Coast all his life, he was reasonably fluent in Spanish but chose not to acknowledge what had been requested. If he played dumb and was indeed about to be kidnapped, then he needed to hold back on some things so that he had a potential element of surprise. It was therefore no surprise to him when one of the brothers returned to the bar with a sack, but Roger chose to fake his expression accordingly.

"We put this on, yes?" indicated Carlos.

"Okay, I suppose, but let me call my colleagues to let them know I am leaving with some friends."

"Sure!" responded Carlos, with a grin that illuminated his face.

Roger took his phone from inside his jacket pocket and hit a pre-programmed number.

"Hi. Look, I'll be leaving with a couple of guys shortly. They're going to show me something that I am keen to see but I'm not to know where it is. So, I'm not being kidnapped!"

There were words said from the other end of the conversation and Roger ended the call as if the process had been pre-arranged.

"Okay, ready when you are!" indicated Roger to his potential kidnapper.

Carlos took the sack from his brother and placed the material over Roger's head so that it concealed his face and part of his shoulders. He was then carefully escorted from the bar with both Carlos and one of his brothers taking a balancing position on either side of him. Whilst Roger couldn't see anything, he was aware that his restricted vision had got brighter and so assumed that they were now exiting the shade of the bar. He couldn't hear any screaming from other people in the street outside, so obviously kidnapping was an activity that aroused no suspicion at all. Perhaps he had made a big mistake in trusting Carlos.

"We step down here, yes?" said Carlos, carefully guiding his catch down a step and onto the main street. As he did so, Roger realised that limping Carlos was on his right.

If he was truly being kidnapped then he would be dragged away from the bar rather than escorted. Perhaps all was well.

It was evident that the other brother had arranged for a vehicle to be parked outside, as Roger could hear an erratic engine ticking over. He felt a hand placed on his head and a gentle push into a slightly warm leather seat. He was soon joined by the two men who seemed to take up a position either side of him.

"We go, yes?" said Carlos.

"We go!" replied Roger.

The vehicle rattled off, bellowing dust from the tyres, and proceeded to journey along the main street, which Roger guessed was no more than fifty metres long. There were then a series of left and right turns, which he tried to place in his memory, but after too many right-hand turns, he realised that his 'captors' were probably trying to confuse his senses before taking the correct route. Roger guessed that he was probably going in the opposite direction to that originally taken and thereafter decided to not bother with trying to memorise the route. He decided to make conversation instead.

"Is it far?" was the best he could muster.

"Oh, far enough to be too far, and not far enough to need an overnight stay on route!" replied Carlos.

Roger realised that Carlos had developed a sense of humour too and that gave him a degree of comfort.

"It's thirty minutes, unless we get a landslide," predicted

Carlos.

Roger sat back and resigned himself to half an hour of an irregular bumpy ride to somewhere that he estimated would be approximately twenty miles away. There was various small talk along the journey about the heat, the insects, life and farming, and in general terms, about politics and religious beliefs of the local population. The small talk succeeded in shortening the apparent distance and time relationship of their journey, and it was with some surprise that Carlos indicated for the vehicle to stop.

"Okay, we here now. I suggest you get your sunglasses ready."

If Carlos and his brothers were seasoned kidnappers, then they were proving to be remarkably considerate ones. Roger therefore reached into his inner jacket pocket and retrieved a pair of designer sunglasses, which he held in both hands, and tucked the arms up under his cloth helmet and onto the bridge of his nose.

"You ready?" enquired Carlos.

"Yep!" responded Roger, and with his affirmation Carlos removed the cloth covering.

Carlos was right to warn his new friend of the impending blast of light, as Roger needed to squint, despite his face being adorned with the best possible eyewear.

After a few seconds he was ready to get out of the vehicle and to follow Carlos up a narrow jungle path of about fifty metres. At the end of the path was a small clearing, that measured approximately twenty metres by about ten metres, and just off centre was a piece of plant matting that presumably covered the entrance to the cavern. This was confirmed by one of the brothers, who was busy arranging a two-piece ladder which he slotted together in anticipation of Carlos requesting an unveiling ceremony. Carlos nodded and the brother duly obliged by pulling back the covering to reveal a small hole just wide enough for a torso and a ladder. The ladder was lifted into the air in fully erect form and slid down into the hole. There was a thud as the base hit the floor, leaving about two rungs showing above ground. Carlos pulled a small torch from his trouser pocket and indicated for Roger to follow him towards the ladder. Roger obliged and peered into the dark cavern beneath. He removed his sunglasses to get a better view and in doing so noticed the faint mauve hue that had greeted him earlier in the bar.

Carlos proceeded to clamber down the ladder with a degree of dexterity that was far too efficient for a man with only one fully functioning leg, and he beckoned Roger to do the same, and the two men had soon disappeared into the underworld.

"Ready?" said Carlos, indicating that he was about to switch on the light show.

"Ready," mirrored Roger.

Carlos flicked the switch on his torch and the whole cavern burst into a magical mauve display of shimmering dancing light that would subtly change shades as Carlos moved the torch around the cavern. Every so often the light would hit a crystal at an exact angle which would project the image that Roger had witnessed in the bar. There would be a black line with equidistant mauve bars either side of it. There were crystals of varying size, from the junior level that Carlos had as a souvenir, up to parent versions that stood about a half a metre tall. There were thousands of them, all standing at various degrees of attention, and which filled the cavern. Roger couldn't determine exactly how far the display journeyed.

"You like?" enquired Carlos.

"I like!" was the natural response from Roger.

There followed a period of silence whilst Roger took in the full vista and he proceeded to do some calculations in his head. Being a seasoned negotiator, he knew how to ask open-ended questions that would take him to the next level of interaction with his new friend.

"So, is there a 'Mrs Carlos'? And a junior 'Carlos'?" enquired Roger.

"No Mrs Carlos but I have two bambinos; Maria and Luis. Luis is in army and Maria is training to be an air force pilot in your country."

"Really?! Where abouts is she and how long has she been doing that?" was the follow up question.

"She in California. Actually, she is a qualified pilot but next month she should pass into the high precision arena and fly fighter jets for a living. I don't see much of her but she writes and phones when she can. She actually wants to be an astronaut and has always had a passion for all things to do with space travel. Her first real birthday present was a telescope. She never wanted girly books about Disney princesses or ponies; just books on the Solar System."

There was a slight block of emotion in his voice as he finished the sentence and Roger let him reflect on what he thought was a lonely family life, but eventually reached into each of his jacket pockets before retrieving a small notebook and a corresponding small pen. He threw in a killer question:

"Would you like to see more of your kids and have the

money to do whatever you want?"

There was a look of surprise on his friend's face as the emotion of separation gave way to an expression of curiosity. He didn't respond verbally but twitched a few facial muscles in acceptance.

Roger continued with his quest:

"Okay Carlos, I can make you very rich," and with that ground-breaking statement he tore three small pieces of paper from the notebook. He gave two pieces to Carlos and kept the third for himself. He handed Carlos the pen before declaring his position:

"Right, I want you to write on one piece of paper what you think your farmland is worth. Don't show it to me but fold it and place it on the floor. On the other piece write the amount you would accept from me to buy your land. Again, don't show it to me and fold that too and place it on the floor. I will write on my bit of paper the amount I will pay you. If my figure is larger than what you have indicated that you want for the farmland, then you agree to sell it to me; all in US dollars. If not, I'll thank you for your time and you can kidnap me again and return me to the town. Do we have a deal?"

Roger held out his hand to seal the deal in the traditional manner and Carlos hesitated before mirroring his actions but, slightly confused, he repeated the terms to ensure that he had heard the proposition correctly.

"You want to buy my farmland for a price that I can possibly set, rather like tossing a coin. I either win or you lose!" chuckled Carlos in confirmation.

"Yes, I suppose you could view it that way," responded Roger, realising that he was close to securing a deal.

"Okay, we do," exclaimed Carlos, writing the first of two figures on the pieces of paper, which he duly folded and placed on the floor in front of him. He wrote out the second number, folded the paper and matched its location to the other piece of paper. He handed Roger the pen to complete the process. Roger wrote his figure and folded it but kept hold of the magic number.

"Show me your first figure," said Roger.

Carlos leant down to retrieve the first piece of folded paper, unwrapped it and read the figure out whilst turning the figure towards Roger.

"$100,000."

"Now show me what you will sell it to me for," asked Roger.

Again, Carlos leant down, this time at a slightly obscure angle, reflecting the bad leg that impeded his progress. He unfolded the piece and read aloud the figure, again turning it to face the questioner.

"$1,500,000," he said, with a smile on his face, as if to imply that no fool would pay such a figure for a piece of poor sheep raising hillside and a collection of odd shaped glass.

"Come on, show me your figure!" declared Carlos.

Roger waited a short period whilst the suspense built up inside Carlos, and just when he thought that Carlos would repeat his demand, he unfolded his piece of paper and read aloud:

"$5,000,000."

"You would have paid me $5,000,000 for my land! I should have asked for more! I've short-changed myself!" exclaimed Carlos, who was both happy that he had a buyer but disappointed that he had lost more than he had won.

"No, I will pay you $5,000,000 because that is what I said I would," replied Roger, calming down the situation.

"Why would you pay me more than I want?" was the natural retort.

"I said I would, and you didn't have to show me the crystal in the bar, nor agree to bring me here to show me your land and this collection of geological formations. You didn't have to shake hands on agreeing to sell the land to me either. You trusted me and that trust should be rewarded, and besides, you will now have enough money to change your life and see more of your children. Everyone should see as much of their children as possible; you deserve that."

Carlos lurched forward and hugged Roger. If he hadn't been accepted before, he was now. The embrace lasted for far too long before Roger intervened.

"Give me your address and I'll get my solicitor to send you the paperwork," were the final words in the cave before both men parted and proceeded on their return journey to the natural light. Sunglasses were required again.

Carlos never did find the ram.

CHAPTER TWO
The Five Trillion Dollar Mission

The human race had always been restricted in the quest to explore the Solar System, being limited to a few manned trips to the Moon, and numerous robotic probes and satellites that had journeyed to various points in the Solar System and beyond. There had always been this in-built, almost pre-programmed desire, to visit and ultimately colonise another planet, and Mars had always glowed an inviting orange hue in the night sky.

For centuries technology had advanced, and with each step man had learnt more, and old theories had given way to a new hypothesis as man's vision had become clearer. The perceived water canals on Mars were nothing more than dusty dry creases on the surface, but subsequent exploration had discovered that water had once been present, and even today accounted for 2% of the Martian soil's fabric. So perhaps those canals were indeed water canals of the past. If water was once present on the surface, perhaps it was still present beneath it in greater concentrations, and this tantalising possibility had drawn humankind to finally make the step of sending a human mission to Mars.

Nobody was expecting technology that would project a human instantly to another planet, but the delay in communication had always been the elephant in the room.

A communication delay of approximately fourteen minutes between Earth and Mars, using conventional VHF channels, would mean that any such mission would have to be self-sufficient and react to any problems using their own initiative. But the cavern, that Carlos had fallen into, held the solution. Roger Haines could now conclude his Mariner Twenty project that would put the first humans onto the red planet.

When Roger Haines had ventured into Central America to find Carlos Da Silva, he knew what he was looking for. Whilst he had the technology to build and fund a fully-fledged manned mission to Mars, he didn't have the technology to allow efficient communication, and consequently the further any spacecraft travelled away from Earth, the longer it would take to know what was going on and whether everything was okay with the mission.

The crystals in the cavern, that Roger Haines now owned, had a special and unique quality – apart from the strange hue that was emitted when a light was shone through it at a certain angle. Nobody really understood how those properties worked but, if a perfect uniform crystal was split equally along its longest axis, then whatever one half was subjected to was instantly experienced by its twin, no matter where it was or how far away it was. Consequently, when these half-crystals were used as part of a communication system, a normal conversation could be held; one half was buried into Mariner Twenty's computer communication channel with the matching half secured in Mission Control back on Earth. Likewise, matching crystal halves embedded in camera equipment would also provide instant images back on Earth.

The hypothesis was that the crystals were formed due

to natural processes, but when these were located over the equator, and a certain geological event occurred, then this gave the crystals their Siamese twin like qualities. That geological event was when the North and South poles switched, which occurred every 500,000 to 900,000 years. The crystals didn't have to be over the equator today, but with Continental Drift and plate tectonics active, as long as the crystals were over the equator when the poles switched, then they would hold these qualities forever. All Roger Haines had done was research old theories from ancient civilisations, and plot the movement of the Continents over time to formulate which parts of today's world would most likely produce the unique crystals. He just had to wait for rumours of mysterious caverns to emerge before plotting his course.

The other advantage of using the crystals in verbal or visual communication devices was that any conversation would be completely secure; only the two matching halves could talk to each other. There was no process by which a conversation could be overheard by interception. That, however, was also the weakness in the system, for if one half of a matching crystal set was somehow damaged, then the other half became useless too. For that reason, each crew member had their own crystal communication device that would patch into a matching half back at Mission Control. But for the sake of a further safety net, a conventional VHF system was also imbedded into the individual communication systems. In addition, both the spacecraft and the previously landed survival pods, that would form the basis of the start of humankind's life on the Martian world, were also fitted with the traditional VHF technology.

Over the previous four years a total of nine survival pods

had been deployed and successfully landed on Mars. Each had been given a sequential Mariner number; the Mariner name rights having been purchased and resurrected by Roger Haines. Some thought this a foolish move, likely to end in catastrophe as, up until Roger Haines had made his bold purchase decision, over half of all missions to Mars had ended in failure. Most were lost without ever knowing what had happened to the craft, and with that sort of track record – and with a fourteen-minute communication delay – it was easy to see why manned missions were held back. Fortunately, since resurrecting the Mariner series of adventures, all nine craft had been successfully landed at or near their intended locations.

Each pod held various items, mainly food orientated, self-sufficient items and scientific equipment that would enable the crew of Mariner Twenty to start a new life, for this was to be a one-way mission; the start of human life on the red planet.

Along with food production facilities and water and power generation units, there was also a pod which carried two handling vehicles that would enable the pods to be transported to a central position adjacent to the Mariner Twenty landing site, which was towards the southern pole of Mars. They would have to be located, and because they were sent from Earth before Roger Haines had perfected the crystal communication process, the VHF system would have to be used, together with location drones that would be released by Mariner Twenty like a flock of doves.

The week had finally arrived when Mariner Twenty would circle the Martian planet, before descending to a pre-determined location in the general vicinity of where the pods had landed.

Mission Control was a collective of nervous men and women who sat behind a series of tiered benches. Each hunched operator had a pair of computer screens in front of them, which monitored whatever task they were expected to control. A gigantic series of screens was positioned at the far wall where a theatre-like stage would not look out of place. These provided the staff with a general overview of what was happening with the mission, but the main focus of attention for most onlookers were the six separate screens, positioned together in a 3 by 2 block, which focused on the individual crew members who were securely strapped into their seats, heavily cocooned in light blue space suits and helmets.

Each suit and helmet matched the occupant to their name, which had been etched into the fabric. In addition, each name had a slightly smaller series of letters underneath that declared their main function of the mission; Juan Cortez – Medic, Jon Lightly – Engineer, Susan Brown – Scientist, Phillipe Bertrand- Scientist, Anna Ling – Scientist and Maria Da Silva – Commander.

Roger Haines had been even more generous to Carlos Da Silva than just the $5,000,000; he had researched his daughter and pushed her along the path to apply, and ultimately achieve, the top slot on his Mariner Twenty project. She was the commander and proud to be so. Her father was likewise the proudest of proud parents but also the saddest of sad people, for he would never see his daughter on Earth again. His only personal experience of her would be the odd five-minute father/daughter chats that she would be allowed each day. She knew that she would not be coming back, and he knew that too, and sometimes he had those moments of doubt. Had he not discovered the hidden crystal cave, and Roger Haines hadn't discovered him, then his daughter would still be many kilometres away but at least she would always be on the same planet. Carlos therefore always tried to dispel his sadness with the knowledge that his daughter would be forever in the history files as commander of the first human mission to Mars. That was his consolation…and the $5,000,000.

Maria Da Silva's task was to develop a first base for an eventual human colony on Mars. The previous Mariner spacecraft had hopefully delivered an array of supplies, which would enable an initial simple, but efficient core of self-sufficient building blocks to start the process. Over the coming years further probes would bring an increasing number of such units, and the small planned hamlet would morph into a small village, capable of sustaining a population of about fifty humans.

The trick was to ensure that any hierarchy was maintained in an orderly fashion, and that no new arrivals would jeopardise the project by undermining the good work already carried out. But that would be a human nature problem; the ability of humans to always think there is a better way, like a child rebelling against its parents, or a generation questioning everything that the previous generation had done. For that reason, the future supplies would be sent in greater quantities than any accompanying human cargo, and only when the psychological impact of relative isolation, encroachment and arguments had been fully monitored, would Roger Haines risk sending any further crew. He had to know what required skills he and his team had overlooked; they had sent three scientists but only one engineer. They thought that would be the required initial mix but what if the engineer suffered a catastrophic accident, would the scientists have the required skills to continue the project?

To try and ensure that the human cargo was sane and healthy, each crew member had a crystal embedded into their suits, which would monitor every minute statistic possible. All the information would be fed into both an Earth based team of medics but also into a computer with AI capabilities, that would look for repeating patterns of behaviour, body temperature, blood pressure, oxygen levels and numerous other minutiae of medical information.

Earth based tests had shown that the computer could predict what sort of afternoon an individual crew member would have based on readings of the previous few hours. It also had a canny knack of predicting friction between crew members. It was important to always keep this in check; one rogue moment of madness could kill the whole crew – literally. Maria Da Silva's task was therefore an extremely difficult one. She had to show authority and also compassion in equal measure. The compassion was evident from her previous training with the crew as a unit that had been subjected to numerous tests, both in space conditions and also through computer model exercises. The authority was backed up by the respect that her crew had shown throughout. But if that didn't work, she was the only one that carried a stun gun that was matched to her bio signature. Only she could use it, only she would be in charge.

Roger Haines therefore thought that he had every possibility covered and a corresponding solution available for every occasion, but in most parts of the world there is a 'Murphy's' or 'Sod's' Law that would dictate that if something could go adrift from a plan, then it eventually would. This mission would be no different, but at this stage everything was going according to plan, and neither the six crew members aloft around Mars, nor the myriad of staff at Mission Control on Earth, could ever have imagined what event would occur to test the knowledge limits of humankind.

With each advance that had occurred over the centuries, there was always an additional and unexpected piece of new knowledge that challenged the status quo of accepted scientific theory; the Mariner Twenty mission would uncover the greatest knowledge shift of all time.

CHAPTER THREE
The Landing

"We are down MC," were the comforting words that were relayed through to Mission Control and, as with all such projects, there was the most enormous roar of cheers and clapping that was customary on such adventures. Grown men turned and hugged their nearest colleagues and even Roger Haines felt obliged to turn to his second in command and give her the warmest and most strenuous of hugs.

So engrossed were the team in self-congratulation, nobody noticed the look of relief and joy that was spread across the six faces on the huge display screens. They had to be content with a mere glance at each other, such was the restriction of their harnesses. All involved had achieved the long-awaited plan of landing humans on Mars.

"Congratulations team!" were the responding words from the Ground Commander, which were only just audible above the cacophony of celebration that went on for far too long but which was understandable, as the Mariner project confirmed that the first part of their mission could be declared a success.

Roger eventually let go of his colleague; she could now breathe again, and having been released from his vice-like grip, felt obliged to punch the air as if she was a coiled spring suddenly released from captivity. She looked odd, as if she had been thirty seconds behind everybody else's celebration.

"We did it!" exclaimed Roger, and everybody turned to face him and applaud his presence.

Roger bowed to replicate his appreciation of the team's efforts, but deliberately sought out Carlos Da Silva in the immediate crowd around him and hugged his companion, as if he were a long-lost brother who hadn't been seen in decades. The pair made an amusing sight, such was their mismatch in height, and with Carlos's bad leg tilting him at an unusual angle as if he was trying to escape. He wasn't, but when the pair finally parted there were tears cascading down Carlos's face and he turned to stare at the image of his daughter up on the main screen. He had lost her, but somehow he was so happy.

"Systems check Mariner Twenty," declared the Ground Commander, as if trying to bring the project back on track.

"Systems check all OK, MC," were the required words that were returned.

The craft was down on Mars and all functions were correct. Nobody had to scurry around to find out what error code 1202 was; nobody had to worry about the fuel levels available; this craft was not designed, nor expected, to take off again. Everything was fine.

The sounds of jubilation eventually subsided and the visible forty-person team in Mission Control gradually sat back down at their consoles to resume their workload, which at this stage was really just to confirm that everything was continuing along the designated path. However, there was also a small additional team of observers that were cocooned in an adjacent room.

They overlooked the main stage of events but were shielded

by a darkened window that prevented anybody seeing in. The door to this room was off of the main corridor, which ran around the semi-circular arena of activity, which the public was allowed to see via the numerous communication channels that were beamed to the world via TV or internet providers. The door was marked 'COMPUTER ROOM 6. LEVEL 1 ACCESS ONLY'. As if to confirm the importance of this location, the door had an additional electronic lock. Only a select few were allowed access to this area; Roger Haines was naturally one such person.

The room did indeed house the normal array of computers but the main task was to receive the initial communication feeds from Mariner Twenty and cleanse them should the unexpected occur. There was a two-minute delay before these pieces of information were eventually fed into the public arena below.

Roger Haines couldn't be responsible for broadcasting live scenes of the demise of the Mariner Twenty crew should the craft explode on landing. He had his safety net in place for good reason having been aware of the history of failures of missions to Mars. This room would also allow for private conversations between the individual crew and Mission Control should the need arise, again before any edited version could be passed into the main control room where the media would pick up any sanitised version.

It also offered the possibility to totally censor parts of the mission. Roger Haines could have viewed the landing from computer room 6 and been two minutes ahead of the rest of his team, or he could have received a text two minutes earlier confirming a successful landing, but he needed to be seen and he needed his reaction to be genuine; he therefore chose to be a 'normal' person for this part of the adventure.

The Ground Commander again broke into a pre-rehearsed statement to Mariner Twenty:

"The choice is up to you. If you're up to it, the drones could set about locating the pods today so that you have a designated planned route for tomorrow. We should have enough daylight left…"

The request was cut short as Maria Da Silva interjected:

"Sure MC. We'll send them out shortly to fix locations and report back once we have located them all."

The large screen declared that each of the six crew were now extracting themselves from their seats and starting to arrange for the drones to be launched out into the Martian sky. The task shouldn't take long as it was the first category of importance. The pods contained everything that the crew would need for their permanent stay, but on board there were sufficient supplies to allow a month or two of existence; beyond that and there would be a problem.

Maria Da Silva knew the importance of the task and had already selected herself to exit the spacecraft and be the first human to set foot on Mars. Having briefly exited the main cabin to change into her external spacesuit, she soon reappeared on screen wearing a slightly thicker light blue suit and carrying a matching helmet in her right hand. Her short dark brown hair would soon be cocooned within the confines of the facial enclosure.

She smiled at the on-board camera, with her grin and matching excited dark brown eyes filling the screen back at Mission Control on Earth. She moved out of shot and her image was picked up by a wide-angle camera which viewed the majority of the cabin. She placed the light blue helmet onto her head and two of the crew carried out a check to ensure that all was well with her suit. The checks were completed and another crew member offered a suitcase which contained the tiny drones that were to be the first planned task.

The door to the airlock was opened and Maria Da Silva stepped inside. She turned and smiled to the crew and the watching audience back on Earth, and this concluded the pleasantries; the work started as the door slid closed behind her. The image on screen now switched to an internal view of the airlock and there was a distortion to the picture as the air was balanced out. A red light in the top corner of the image switched colour to green and Maria Da Silva reached forward to place her gloved hand on the large button marked 'open'. There was a further distortion of the picture as the external door flipped down and the autofocus adjusted to the new view; Mars was outside and Maria da Silva would soon be part of it.

She turned around, and in doing so filled the screen with her light blue suit before slowly exiting backwards out of the capsule, using the in-built steps in the outer door to assist her descent. The large screen switched to an external camera and Maria's image was clear for all to see as she gingerly stepped down onto the Martian surface.

There was a small amount of red dust that displaced itself into the air around her right boot, before it settled back down onto the Martian floor. Maria carefully placed her left boot down adjacent to her right one, and briefly stood to attention before turning around to stare at the vista that was in front of her. The large screen again switched images to now show the horizon that was being captured by Maria's body camera. She felt obliged to say something profound but ended up editing what had already been said back in 1969:

"That's one bigger step and one bigger leap for humankind."

She giggled nervously and this was mirrored back at Mission Control as the majority of the staff joined in with her expression of awe.

Maria da Silva took a few more steps away from the body of Mariner Twenty and turned around, looking down at the series of footprints that she had left behind her, which revealed a mixture of orange and black dust. The words 'HAINES INC.' were left embossed into the soil wherever she had placed her boots; Roger Haines had never missed the opportunity to do some self-promotion.

Having taken in the vista, she was ready to release the drones into the sky. She placed the suitcase onto the dust beneath her, and crouching down, flicked open the two extra-large catches which secured the contents. The inside held a dozen small drones, each numbered and each blinking a small light, which indicated that they were charged and ready to fly.

One by one the large screen back at Mission Control received the images from her body camera as she bent down and picked up the first drone. She squeezed the main body of the drone and the four rotors sprang into life, and after holding the item aloft in her hand, she released the machine as if it were a dove released from Noah's Ark. It hovered briefly above her head before presumably latching onto the nearest VHF signal emitted from the most adjacent pod, and it was soon whirring its way across the sky and to its intended location.

Her body camera couldn't keep up with the speed of the miniature drone and the image was soon replaced by a picture of the suitcase, as Maria Da Silva again bent down to retrieve, and ultimately release, the next drone. Again, she held it aloft and squeezed it gently. It too flew off and onto the next location. This time the route was more in line with the front of her body, and so the body camera managed to hold onto the image until it blinked its way out of focus and potentially over the horizon.

She repeated the process numerous times, releasing the drones in numerical order, but so engrossed was she in her new surroundings, she didn't realise that she had actually released ten small drones, rather than the required nine that were intended to locate the corresponding nine survival pods. However, all ten drones had indeed been released into the Martian vista, and both she and Mission Control assumed that the tenth drone would latch onto the nearest VHF signal and would double up with the first drone released. It was therefore no surprise when the first returning pair of drones included drone number one, but it was a surprise when drone three was the companion.

The remaining drones returned to Maria da Silva's position in an orderly fashion, with drone ten being the last to make its appearance. Mission Control could see the journeys that each drone had taken, with their routes being displayed on the large screen back on Earth. Drone ten had indeed initially followed the path of drone one to the nearest pod, but had then taken a sharp right-angled turn and ended up being the furthest away from Mariner Twenty, before eventually returning. Mission Control reported to Maria Da Silva that the task had been successful:

"We think drone ten aborted, as it might have picked up that drone one had already found the position of the nearest pod. Just surprised that it took such a large arced route back to you, but hey, you've located the nine pods. All seem relatively nearby. Drone four located the handling equipment, so we suggest that you get to that one first tomorrow."

"Sure," replied Maria Da Silva, forgetting to use the standard response of 'roger', but with the instant communication equipment there was less chance of misinterpreting something, and so a more natural response was forthcoming. She therefore concluded that this part of her mission was complete and so bent down and continued packing away the drones into the suitcase beneath her. As the rogue drone ten was placed back into its housing, she smiled and muttered:

"You're going to be trouble, aren't you?!"

She then carefully stood upright and turned around to return to the relative comfort of the Mariner Twenty cabin. As she traversed the red Martian soil again, she became mesmerised by the pattern of footprints that she had left behind and felt a warm proud glow inside her. So did Roger Haines, who could see even more images of his company logo imprinted into the Martian soil.

Maria then carefully placed the suitcase back into the spacecraft and proceeded to clamber up the steps that were part of the inside of the door. She was soon inside and pressed her right glove against the door closure button, and with that was the accompanying sound of the metal returning to its frame. The red button glowed large, indicating that she should do something, and consequently she pressed her glove against the required button, which would return the atmosphere inside the chamber to balance that of the main cabin.

A green light glowed, informing her that she could proceed.

The door to the main cabin opened and her colleagues stood clapping at her triumphant return as she entered the arena. She placed the suitcase down on the ground in front of her, and released her helmet from its mooring to reveal a slightly sweaty face, which declared that flying drones on a different planet was not as easy as had been planned.

CHAPTER FOUR
Pod Four

The following day Maria Da Silva was accompanied by Jon Lightly and Anna Ling in the initial quest to recover pod four and return it to the Mariner Twenty landing site. Jon was in his late thirties and was solidly built without being overweight. His reflective visor hid his green eyes and bald head, and such was the smoothness of his featureless dome that the crew had nicknamed him 'Pluto', after the particularly smooth region of the celestial body. Anna, by contrast, was slightly built and the smallest and lightest of the crew. She had long jet-black hair and eyes that almost matched but they were dark brown; darker than Maria Da Silva's, and with more of an inquisitive nature, as if she was always searching for the answer to something that nobody else had considered a question.

The three light blue cocooned individuals slowly marched across the Martian landscape towards the green blip that was presented to them on the inside of their helmets, and which gave the distance and direction details. The technology indicated that pod four was approximately 250 metres away, just on the other side of a shallow ridge that formed the horizon. The ridge was an easy ascent but the corresponding descent down towards pod four was slightly steeper and required the three companions to tread carefully, as the soil underfoot proved to be loose and unstable. However, all three managed to successfully traverse the terrain towards the silver container that was now only about twenty metres in front of them.

There was a sudden flash of light as the roof of solar panels on the pod reflected the sun across their path. A green light on top of the ten-metre-long rectangular unit blinked slowly, which indicated that it had been successfully tagged by drone four. The three approached the final few metres before Jon Lightly broke away from his two colleagues and circled around the back to ensure that the unit was undamaged. He reappeared with a smile beaming through his glass visor and held up his right gloved hand and erected his thumb to indicate that all was well.

Maria Da Silva made the final approach towards the container's visible end, and using her right gloved hand pressed against a backlit square button. There was a slight hiss as the seal around the frame was broken and the front flap slowly tilted towards the ground. As it did so, the inside of the container became illuminated to reveal the contents; two quad-like vehicles parked one in front of the other, both with enclosed cabins and with extendable cranes that projected from the back of each unit and over the front of the vehicles.

The inside of the pod was lined with a plastic padding which was opaque and had the words: 'DO NOT REMOVE' printed at regular intervals along its length. A red hand in a 'stop' position faced the viewer and enhanced the instruction.

The padding contained a volume of water several centimetres deep. Whilst the water was considered drinkable in extreme circumstances, the instruction for the padding and its contents to remain in situ meant that the construction held a more important function; it was a layer of protection. Not only did it potentially absorb any movement of the pod's contents during the flight from Earth and the eventual landing on Mars, it would also protect the Mariner Twenty crew.

Water had been found to be a good and simple form of protection against some of the naturally occurring radiation that bombarded everything in the Universe. The pods, once emptied of their contents, would become the living and working quarters for the crew and they needed to be protected. Water was the simplest solution to a problem that was omni-present, and as Mars didn't have any notable magnetic field that could shield and act as a natural barrier to any radiation, the padding would have to work. Luckily, the padding looked to be intact.

There was just enough room for the thinnest of the three companions to squeeze past the front quad, and this was confirmed as Jon Lightly and Maria Da Silva both glanced in unison at Anna Ling, thereby inviting her to perform the first task. She duly approached the right-hand side of the container and positioned herself into a sideways, crab-like stance and slowly edged past the front of the first quad, her light blue space suit gently rubbing against the pod's internal padding. Having reached the side of the quad cabin she reached forward and pressed against the side of its door, which hissed as it slowly slid up towards the ceiling of the container. The inside of the cabin illuminated the interior of both the quad itself and the container, and as the light bounced around inside it became evident that the colour scheme of the quads matched the light blue hue of the spacesuits.

Anna Ling carefully placed her right leg onto a conveniently engineered step that was built into the side of the quad and heaved herself into the cabin. She pulled down on the door and became one with the quad. The interior light in the cabin extinguished itself and was replaced by a slightly lower concentration of luminescence. She looked forward towards her two colleagues and awaited the signal to start the exiting procedure. The two light blue figures both stepped away from the container and raised their thumbs to indicate that they were ready to receive the first of their new toys.

Anna Ling glanced around her and pressed the large illuminated 'start' button. There was a whirring that emanated from somewhere beneath the cabin, but which became a deafening din as it reverberated around the inside of the container. She decided to speed up the process to escape the noise, which was becoming unpleasant, and so pressed the release button that de-magnetised the unit, and which had secured the quad during the flight from Earth and the subsequent landing on Mars. She quickly moved the motion lever forward, took her left hand off of the brake lever on the steering wheel column, and the quad subsequently edged forward and out of the container, revealing its splendid light blue colour scheme. She encircled her two companions and eventually parked the quad away from the container and allowed the Martian dust to settle.

Her task wasn't over yet as the back quad also required her slight frame to remove it. She consequently removed herself from the pod's cabin and as she exited beckoned Jon Lightly to take her place. Anna then marched slowly back into the container to clamber past the front of the other quad and into its cabin. Again, the inside of the container glowed with the warm light emitted from the quad cabin, and this was soon followed by the familiar whirring sound which was even louder than the first occasion. Anna Ling didn't waste any time in completing the exit process and the second quad was soon outside of its home and ready for the next task.

Maria Da Silva slowly edged towards the container door frame and again pressed the large button on the outside, which returned the flap back into its intended location. She waved her hands towards her two colleagues who took up the instruction to proceed to each end of the empty container.

Jon Lightly moved his quad towards the hidden rear of the container, and in doing so extended the crane further over the cabin, so that it was now protruding a good two metres in front of him. The business end of the crane's shaft held a large pair of pincers that extended outwards to a pre-determined width, and which enabled it to grab tightly around the body of the container.

Anna Ling performed an identical manoeuvre but positioned her crane behind her and reversed her quad towards the front of the container. Both quad cranes locked their pincers around the container and almost in unison lifted the empty unit from the ground. There was a small cloud of red dust that settled underneath where the container had been, and once Maria Da Silva was satisfied that the unit was sufficiently clear of the ground, she proceeded towards Anna Ling's quad and joined her in the adjacent seat.

Anna Ling pressed the centre of the steering wheel, which resulted in two short beeps being broadcast to the area, and which indicated that they were ready to move off. Jon Lightly would just be a rear passenger, pushing the container forward whilst the front quad did the directional work and pulling capacity. There was a subsequent large cloud of red dust that filled the immediate area as both quads battled through the loose soil and back towards the Mariner Twenty landing site.

Despite the numerous tests of the quad's capabilities over all sorts of terrains back on Earth, the lack of Martian atmosphere was always going to test the limits of the workhorses. To be safe, Maria Da Silva pointed to a less severe slope to be taken, and in no time the articulated convoy was up over the ridge and in sight of their colleagues back at base. The red cloud of dust mirrored their progress, eventually settling somewhere behind them and back to relative stability.

About ten metres from Mariner Twenty, the small convoy came to a halt and a subsequent cloud of red dust fell back to the ground. Again, two short beeps were heard emanating from the front quad and this signalled for the pair of quads to lower their cargo ends and release their grips. The two quads then slowly manoeuvred to a position either side of the empty container.

Rather than return to the safety of the Mariner Twenty cabin, the two quads set off in the opposite direction from where they had been and proceeded to locate the next pod. Once more the details of the location were projected onto the inside of the trio's visors, and all the remaining crew could do was trace the journey by the column of red dust that accompanied the explorer's path.

No pods were physically visible from Mariner Twenty, and so the only indication that another pod had been located was when the column of dust eventually stopped and the sky cleared, as this indicated that something had stopped happening, and something more strenuous was taking place.

Within thirty minutes the dust was again visible on the horizon, and the red mist grew in intensity as the pair of quads carried another survival pod back to the new colony. This too was carefully placed adjacent to the existing empty pod and the convoy again set off for a third pod retrieval exercise. Again, a cloud of dust chased their movements over the horizon and within a similar time frame the trio of explorers returned with another pod, which again was placed in what was now the unofficial unloading area.

"Call it a day, Maria," was heard inside her helmet, as Mission Control judged that the trio were over-exerting themselves, doubtless due to the medical information being received back on Earth, indicating that too much energy was being spent.

"Roger," replied Maria Da Silva, who had returned to normal protocol mode.

CHAPTER FIVE
Tell the World

The adjacent conference room to the main Mission Control complex was full of expectant questioners. This was to be the first of several press conferences where journalists from all sides of the planet would be able to ask uncensored questions about how the mission was progressing and where it was going.

The ground rules had already been laid down by Roger Haines and his associates, which effectively had set a system of fairness into the procedure. Basically, each of the numerous reporters had been allocated a sequential number, which was also embossed into their identity badge that was to be worn at all times. Journalist number one would start the procedure; they would be able to ask two questions before the second journalist was given the same opportunity, and then journalist number three, until the hour-long allotted meeting was used up. The next press conference would continue with the next journalist starting the questioning.

There was nothing off limits, but if the answer to the question involved some trade secrets being declared, then Roger Haines had the ability to veto. All the journalists had signed up to this rule. It was anticipated that journos who had asked earlier questions, would perhaps gauge when their next day for an opportunity would occur, and prepare follow up questions to previous topics asked from the gathering. Roger Haines therefore anticipated that there would be a bit of backwards and forwards in the nature of the questions.

The backdrop to the room had an enormous image screen which filled the entire back wall. The screen held the iconic image from the day before; Maria Da Silva's boot print, which declared that HAINES INC. effectively owned that portion of Mars. In front of the iconic declaration was a long table, behind which Roger Haines and four of his experienced colleagues were seated. There were the customary name plates and bottled water in front of each of them, and in front of the stage was a collection of experienced journalists and an accompanying cacophony of numerous conversations that filled the void.

"Good Morning, people!" declared Roger Haines, and in doing so the noise of chatter subsided to a respectful silence as the masses awaited the opening salvo. Roger Haines continued:

"Okay, so you all know the rules for being here. We will start with journo one, who will be allowed to ask two questions, and then we proceed onto number two and so on, until the hour-long session is concluded. We then start from where we left off on the following occasion. Okay?"

There was a collective sound of approval and so Roger Haines continued with the task:

"Okay, first on our list is Steve Jones from *The New York Times*. Steve, go ahead."

Steve Jones duly stood up from his seated position near the front of the auditorium to announce his presence, and used the required questioning process, which was namely to speak into his own phone. The technology embedded in the room allowed the question to be broadcast direct from the numerous speakers that were dotted around the auditorium, so that both the rest of the audience and the panel on stage could hear. The technology also allowed those with limited English to both ask a question, and receive the answer, in their native tongue via a complex auto translate algorithm which held all the main languages of the world.

"Thanks, Roger," responded the questioner before continuing:

"I noted that when Maria, Jon and Anna were retrieving the pods yesterday that they were only using hand signals and glances to communicate with each other. Was there a problem with the internal VHF system that the crew would normally use?"

Roger glanced along the table before volunteering the answer that he knew was correct:

"Thanks, Steve for your question. No, there was nothing wrong with the VHF communication system. Basically, we were playing safe as the pods rely on the same system. Having located all of the pods, we didn't want to possibly interfere and corrupt their collection by introducing another series of VHF communications, which may have distorted their whereabouts. I know we have them logged, but there was a danger that we would turn off the VHF beacons if we introduced another set of communications, and we didn't want to complicate our position. Maria and the team will be using that channel when we have all the pods back. Is that okay, Steve?"

Steve nodded before asking his second allotted question:

"Also, we saw that Maria let an extra tenth drone go out on reconnaissance, which I appreciate was probably her getting carried away with being the first person on Mars, but do we know why it did such a large detour route on returning home?"

Roger Haines looked along the line of his colleagues and nodded to Susie Letts, Communications Technician, to provide a response, which she duly obliged.

"Steve, thanks for that. Yes, it took a rather unusual curved route back to Maria. You'll appreciate that these drones are autonomous and are basically there to latch onto a VHF signal. Once they have located their required pod, this sets off a beacon on the pod that registers it is unavailable to be found again. The next drone released then finds the next nearest pod, and so on, until all the pods are located. We think that drone ten may have actually picked up a VHF signal from the returning drone one, and when it realised that it was on a potential collision course with its brother, it took avoiding action and entered into a safety mode which put it a safe distance away by taking a looped route."

Steve nodded in acceptance.

Roger Haines then looked down at his list for the next two-question volunteer.

"Lorraine Questa from *Heraldo de Madrid.*"

Lorraine made herself visible by standing proudly at the rear of the auditorium. Roger thought that this would be the first use of the auto-translate aspect of the hall's facilities, but in a perfect English accent Lorraine asked her question:

"Susie, following on from the last question about the drones, if they are used just for locking onto the pods, then isn't that a bit of a waste, as once they are retrieved then they'll just be scrap, won't they?"

Susie continued conveying her knowledge of 'all things

drone.'

"Actually, they can be used again in two ways. Firstly, when we send further pods, then they will also need to be located and the drones will be used then, but also there is a glorified *Mecanno* set in one of the pods that can be used. The crew can bolt on the drones to the frame and use it to move small bits of kit around; actually, there is also a lightweight seat that can be suspended underneath the frame which can carry a crew member."

Lorraine nodded acceptance and proceeded with her follow up question:

"So, when will the next pods be sent, noting that it will take numerous months for anything to get there?"

Roger decided to rescue Susie.

"Well, it does indeed take a very long time to get anything to Mars, but first we have to ascertain what the crew may need which we have overlooked, and what they may actually need because one of the pods is damaged and the contents too badly compromised. The crew have only retrieved a third of the pods, so we won't know for a couple of weeks yet what they actually will require. We think we have supplies ready to go for everything they may need but I am afraid at the moment it is a case of known unknowns rather than anything else."

"Okay, who's next?" remarked Roger Haines. "It looks like Robert Coyne from *The London Times*. Go ahead, Robert."

Robert Coyne made himself known to the panel. He was situated near the front but slightly to one side.

"Is there anything that has surprised you about the mission so far; either good or bad?"

Roger Haines looked at his adjacent colleague, Colin

Green; his name plate declared that he was Chief Scientist at Mission Control.

"Robert, I think we have been pleasantly surprised at how the landing went without any problems, and also that Maria and her team have managed to locate all of the nine survival pods. I appreciate that they haven't physically recovered them all yet, and so we don't know what state they are in, nor the contents for that matter, but so far so good. On the negative side, I think we are surprised at the ease at which the Martian dust is disturbed, and I suppose my worry is that the crew will probably be doing a lot of dusting!"

There was a collective giggle around the room and a collection of smiles on the stage. Robert Coyne continued with his second question:

"Thanks Colin. What problems do you think there may be going forward with any relationships between the individual crew members?"

Roger immediately glanced in the direction of Charles Linton, who was the Groups Head Psychologist. Roger knew that Charles's expertise would come in handy one day, and here was his chance for fame, as he had already anticipated this sort of question and had a lengthy reply just waiting to be told to the world:

"Thanks for your question, Robert. Okay, where to start? Can I first say that it is not the intention for this group of crew members to engage in any human reproduction. They were not chosen for their breeding potential but rather their ability to work together in an alien environment. One of the early stages of selection involved the hundred or so candidates being tested on the attractiveness of the other candidates, via a confidential test using videos and still photos. From this we could ascertain where any attraction resided – either singular or mutual – and try and avoid putting these people together on this part of the project. We think we have achieved that. Now, as we all know, whilst there is instant attraction, there is also the possibility of mutual attraction developing over time, as there is in any working environment, but these guys will be in a confined space with nowhere to run to if things develop. So, I appreciate that over time we may see closeness develop between people. I don't want to see it, and we have an action plan if we see the inklings of anything. Remember that each crew member has a half-crystal embedded in their under suit which monitors all of their medical functions, and that data can be used to see if something is happening that shouldn't be. At some stage in the future we will be sending pre-developed pairs up to Mars. Part of their function will be to breed and start to develop a true human colony on the Martian surface. We are some way from sending those people but that part of the project is ongoing, and we have so much else to do up there before we can think about a formal breeding program. Indeed, the next couple of trips will likely involve further people who have the skills that we may notice are necessary from any gaps we see in this initial mission. I would also say that this lot are going to be extremely busy and hopefully will be too tired for any of that nonsense."

There was again a collective giggle as Charles Linton finally finished his sermon. Roger Haines looked relieved, as did the original questioner, who had out of politeness remained standing during the entire reply.

"Right, we now have Giorgi Lustav from *Europe Today Magazine*. Giorgi can we have your questions please?"

Giorgi Lustav leapt up, as if his whole morning had been anticipating that he would be called in the first press conference, rather than being relegated to a subsequent day when perhaps the action hadn't been as exciting.

Giorgi chose to see if the auto-translate system would actually work and so declared his questions in his native Russian. He therefore spoke into his phone, and near instantly his question was broadcast to the room in perfect English.

"Sorry, but my English is okay for ordering a coffee or asking where the station is, but for this sort of technical scientific stuff, I think I need to speak in Russian."

There was an appreciative nod from the room that Giorgi had owned up to probably not being able to understand any answer. He therefore didn't persist in entertaining the gathered crowd with his version of the English language.

"Okay, so why did you decide to have your company name embossed into the soles of the boots?"

As the question was asked, Giorgi nodded his head in the direction of the huge screen behind the panel that had indeed been displaying the image. Roger Haines felt obliged to answer, and as he did so, Giorgi held his phone closer to his ear as the Russian version was relayed to him.

"Giorgi, thanks for your question. As you'll appreciate, we have invested trillions of dollars in planning and developing this project, and I suppose there is a bit of vanity in me seeing my company logo etched into the Martian soil. It will be covered in time with red dust but I appreciate and accept that it may be unsavoury to some people, but I would also mention that when the USA put Armstrong and Aldrin on the Moon, they put up the American flag. They could have put the United Nations flag there instead, but there was a huge degree of pride that had to be cemented and celebrated, and I don't think I am being much different."

Giorgi nodded and proceeded with his subsequent question:

"I appreciate that this is meant to be a one-way mission, with the crew eventually ending their lives on Mars, but is there an escape method should things go wrong and it would be better to extract the crew from the planet?"

Roger Haines looked slightly troubled by this question, as he didn't want to think that the project would go so bad as to have to retrieve the crew, but nevertheless Giorgi had asked a relevant question and he deserved a reply, and so Roger volunteered one:

"Giorgi, you are correct that we are not planning to bring the crew back to Earth. They signed up on that basis and are accepting of the fact that they will eventually die up there. However, if things got bad – let's say they are attacked by aliens – then we can get Mariner Twenty to take off and rendezvous with the orbiting main rocket which delivered them to Mars. That would enable the crew to start a flight back to Earth, but they would have to be met part-way by another craft for them to complete their journey home. There simply isn't enough fuel to get them back. I would also mention that when we sent them up to Mars the distance between the two planets was at its shortest, but as you will know, depending on the orbit of both Mars and Earth, there can be huge variations in the distances between the two, and consequently in the time taken for any return journey. I believe the distance can vary by over one hundred million kilometres between the shortest and longest distances between the two planets. There is also the problem of supplies for such a journey. An alternative plan would be for Mariner Twenty to take a short trip to either Phobos or Deimos, taking some of the scientific equipment with them, and await a suitable window of opportunity before heading back. Not a simple task and not one we want to be dealing with if at all possible."

That quietened the crowd, and with that pause Roger Haines glanced at his watch and suggested that they end the press conference there as their time slot was nearly completed.

"Okay, next time we'll start with Pierre Fons from *La Monde*."

With that final statement the crowd of journalists stood to their feet, and there was the usual rumble of individual conversations that filled the room as the panel left for more important things.

As Roger Haines stepped down from the podium there was a 'ping' on his phone. He looked down and read the very simple message, which just said '6'. Roger Haines knew what that meant, and he quickly brushed past his colleagues and up the stairs that would take him to the mysterious computer room 6.

Having reached the first-floor corridor, Roger Haines hurried along the semi-circular structure that overlooked the main control room. He arrived at computer room 6 and held his ID card against one of the necessary electronic plates; it turned green and allowed Roger to place his phone against the second plate. There was an electronic click and the door opened allowing him to enter the hidden domain of secrecy.

The room held a bank of computers and a corresponding row of joined desks facing the main Mission Control below them. Four people sat at the desks monitoring the various screens that held the numerous live feeds from the cameras on Mars. One of the chairs swung around to face Roger Haines as he edged further into the room.

"Thanks for coming so quickly but I thought you'd want to know this after the press conference rather than before."

The voice was matched to a grey-haired gentleman of slim build and with a southern US accent. The room was fairly dark, and so the definitive facial features of the speaker were not truly visible until Roger's eyes had adjusted to his surroundings.

"What's up?" responded Roger.

"Okay, so when the drones were released yesterday, ten went out instead of the planned nine. All ten returned after having latched onto a VHF signal."

The voice awaited Roger Haines querying that statement as he would only be aware that nine had correctly matched with a signal.

"How so? I thought drone ten just veered away and avoided colliding with one of the others."

"It did veer away but it veered away to lock onto another signal. A weak signal but a signal nevertheless."

Roger Haines looked puzzled but ploughed on with his questions:

"So, what did it latch onto? Did one of the survival pods break into two pieces?"

The voice now had a relatively youthful face which didn't match the grey hair that surrounded it, but responded in a manner that imparted a surprise:

"We don't know what it latched onto, and it can't be two parts of the same pod as there is only one VHF system attached to each one."

"Could it be the same pod broken in two but somehow the VHF signal is bouncing off of the other part?"

"Doubtful, as it's too far away from any of the other pods. It's a new signal. We removed the blip from the screen but kept the route taken, as let's face it, the world knew that ten drones were dispatched so they would be expecting ten routes to be plotted. Or the tenth drone not returning at all because it got confused and crashed. The answer given at the press conference was perfectly viable and it looks as though the internet population has accepted it."

Roger Haines metaphorically scratched his head and felt obliged to ask the man what to do:

"So, what should we do; should we tell the crew, or Maria at least?"

The young faced voice was quick to respond as if anticipating the question:

"No. Let them retrieve all nine pods first and when they have started the building project, we'll get Maria to send out one of the camera drones to the general area. The rest of the team will be busy and we can perhaps keep them out of the loop, but Maria will have to be brought into the inner circle on this."

"Okay, agreed, and we keep to the story said downstairs, yes?"

"Yep," was the confirmation.

Roger Haines felt obliged to ask one other question:

"Is there anything else I should know; are there any other foibles out there?"

"That's all we have so far, but don't worry if anything else crops up I'll give you notice of it."

Roger Haines composed himself before turning around and walking towards the door. He again placed his ID card against the necessary plate adjacent to the door frame and awaited the request to place his phone against another electronic plate. There was a satisfying click as the door revealed the outside corridor.

CHAPTER SIX
More Pods

Maria Da Silva awoke early, and having consumed a breakfast meal that looked as though it had already been eaten, she gathered her five colleagues around for a morning briefing. Today would be the day when they would attempt to retrieve the remaining six survival pods. There was no need for diagrams on white boards or fancy graphics on computers; the task was simple enough, just follow the images on the inside of their helmet visors to the six different locations, and return the pods to what was now known as 'Red Base'.

Whilst it was considered preferable to give the three static crew members a chance to drive the quads, Maria Da Silva was happier using Anna Ling and Jon Lightly, who had previously demonstrated their skills admirably, so her decision was not penalising the other crew members but using the known skills of Anna and Jon. All seemed to be in agreement and so the trio got changed into their outside work suits and entered the air lock to start the task.

Again, there would be no verbal communication between the team due to the VHF restriction that they had placed on this initial part of the project. The hand signals had been sufficient previously and they would be so again. Maria Da

Silva suggested that they head towards the next nearest pod, and so eventually the two quads journeyed off leaving a plume of red dust in their wake. The remaining three crew members looked out of the small Mariner Twenty windows and watched the red trail disappear into the distance.

After about twenty-five minutes the dust started to settle and there was again a clear view of the horizon. The absence of any dust in the visible air implied that the team had reached their destination, and so it was no surprise that forty minutes later the cloud of red dust indicated that Maria, Anna and Jon were on their return leg.

The red dust cloud grew larger and eventually the flashes of light blue quad casing appeared in ever larger portions, as the vehicles proceeded nearer and nearer to Red Base, and the amount of dust was overtaken by the size of the quads themselves. The convoy pulled up to a stop adjacent to the existing three pods, unloaded their catch and journeyed off in another direction to recover the fifth pod. Again, the red dust cloud indicated that the team were on the move, and again after about an hour they returned with another unit, which was unloaded in the unofficial parking lot. A sixth pod recovery journey followed and that pod was retrieved and parked. By now over three hours had elapsed and Maria Da Silva was conscious that she and her team should take a rest, so the quads were parked up and the three escapees returned to the air lock and the eventual sanctuary of the Mariner Twenty interior.

It was evident that at some point they should actually look inside and investigate what they had retrieved, and whether the contents were intact and usable.

Whilst each pod was marked on the outside with the general

contents – food prep, living quarters, lab etc., it would still be like Christmas Day when the contents were finally unwrapped. The design for the pod landings had involved both parachutes and reverse thrusters. There was also a spring-loaded internal floor that, together with the other safety features, should have enabled the contents to be protected as much as possible. The quads themselves had survived the descent and so the crew were hopeful that all the other pod's contents had survived too. To combat the boredom, Maria Da Silva suggested that two of the remaining three crew members should perhaps perform a stock taking task, whilst Maria and her team collected the final three survival pods.

A brief lunch of pre-chewed food and scientific conversation was followed by the re-instatement of the retrieval task, and the trio of explorers were soon on their next departure, leaving Phillipe Bertrand, Juan Cortez and Susan Brown to rotate tasks whilst stock taking. Protocol dictated that not all of the crew should be outside of Mariner Twenty at the same time, and consequently it was up to Juan Cortez to remain cocooned, whilst his colleagues performed the task of opening each of the pods, and noting what was still intact and what would have to be repaired.

Juan decided to ease his potential boredom by playing chess against the on-board computer and, being the mission medic, he had the unenviable task of hopefully never being needed. His days would therefore be spent playing computer chess and generally assisting the others. There was some debate as to whether a medic was needed at all, as medical direction could be given from Mission Control on Earth, but after several discussions it was thought wise to send an experienced overseer who could give hands-on remedies. His mid-thirties age defied his actual abilities, as Juan Cortez had seen action in war zones, industrial complexes and general medical hospitals, and he had a pleasing bedside manner, probably assisted by his healthy, lightly tanned complexion and sympathetic mid-brown eyes.

As Phillipe Bertrand and Susan Brown opened the first of the pods, it became evident that the food production facilities that would be so vital for their survival, had indeed been spared any disruption. The water treatment and recycling equipment, which took up about a half of the pod, had been well protected and well packaged, and whilst they couldn't be sure that all was well until they actually pressed a few buttons, the signs were hopeful. As were the encapsulated supply of seedlings and already sprouting plants that looked splendidly healthy in the reflected internal light of the pod. It looked as though they wouldn't be dying on Mars from starvation; radiation poisoning or some exotic Martian disease, maybe, but not from starvation if all went well with the food production aspect of their mission.

The next pod was marked 'LAB'. This would hopefully hold a range of scientific equipment that would enable the three scientists to analyse and discover numerous aspects of the Martian environment in a real time scenario. Although previous Martian robotic probes had sampled soil and air constituents, there were limitations to what could be achieved by such methods. A real scientist on site would be able to discover so much more. The two per cent water aspect of the soil, which had been previously analysed by robotic probes, could only measure within a limited geographic area, whereas the crew of Mariner Twenty had the prospect of travelling further afield in the hope that perhaps there was a higher concentration of water elsewhere. This was anticipated to be a likely discovery at the South Pole, or maybe in underground caverns that had always been anticipated to hold liquid water, but had yet to be proven. There was consequently a huge amount of anticipation as Phillipe held out his right gloved hand and pressed it firmly against the illuminated button which would enable the contents to be revealed.

There was the customary 'hiss' as the seal was broken and the front flap slowly lowered itself towards the ground. The internal light illuminated the contents which were all neatly stacked and strapped into their rightful places. The two scientists looked at each other and smiled in unison at the sight that their working tools were intact. Susan activated her visor cam and was instantly presented with the contents of the pod. The list was projected onto the inside of her visor; there was no need for her to go cross-eyed as the technology physically focused the image to appear about half a metre in front of her, as if she was reading a manual. She was looking for something in particular, and soon she could confirm that her chosen comfy scientific chair was indeed somewhere in the pod. She smiled to herself and the pair moved onto the next adjacent pod, which was also marked 'LAB'. There was a lot of scientific work to do on this mission.

Again, Phillipe Bertrand held out a gloved hand and pressed it against the illuminated button that would enable exploration of the next 'Aladdin's Cave'. The hiss of seal breakage was accompanied by the illumination of the contents and again all seemed well. This time Phillipe illuminated the contents onto a list in front of his visor. He nodded appreciatively, as even though there was a third 'LAB' pod somewhere, the two intact pods would enable them to carry out an array of scientific work. He didn't care what chair he had to sit on, as long as there was an actual chair; and there was.

The excitement of unwrapping Christmas presents was interrupted by the sight on the horizon of another red dust column. Maria Da Silva and her team were on the way back with another package for them to explore. Phillipe decided to close the pod doors to prevent an avalanche of red dust entering his pristine pods, and so reaching out a gloved hand, he pressed the illuminated buttons that would seal the contents once again.

The red dust cloud grew larger as the first actual signs of the front quad vehicle became visible. The pair could soon see the individual outlines of Maria and Anna sitting adjacent to each other in the now slowing motion of confusion. The convoy slowed to a reasonable pace and then stopped, allowing the occupants to detach the pod that they were carrying, but they were then engulfed in a downpour of red dust as the swirling vortex of material caught up with them. It soon settled leaving a thin film of red over everything in the area.

The five crew members were close enough to be able to smile a confirming expression of acceptance to each other, and with Maria Da Silva in a hurry to complete the collection of containers, she had soon instructed her part of the team to journey off to the next location, which again was projected onto the inside of their visors.

This time the two quads took off in a more sedate manner, allowing Phillipe Bertrand and Susan Brown to re-start their task with the minimum of red fog. The two quads then hurtled off once they had cleared the area, and again the swirl of red dust plotted their progress across the Martian landscape and towards their next target.

Susan's vision followed the dust storm over a ridge and presumably down the other side and onwards towards wherever the next pod was located. The top of the dust plume got smaller and smaller in intensity as Maria Da Silva's team drove further and further away from Red Base. This was the furthest trip so far by some considerable distance. Susan and Phillipe returned to the task of stock taking and proceeded to complete the arduous, and by now less exciting, unwrapping of their Christmas presents. Tedium had set in for them both.

After over an hour of checking contents, the pair had finally completed their stocktake of all the pod's interior supplies; all was well and there was a degree of relieved satisfaction at the finality of what they had achieved. They stood back to mentally re-arrange the pods into their eventual configuration. The plan was to construct the pods into two 'X' patterns, which would be connected by one of the arms of each 'letter'. The ninth pod would be separate and would continue to be used as storage for the two quads.

Of concern, however, was that Maria Da Silva's convoy had not returned, and it was therefore a relief when eventually a plume of red dust was seen on the horizon. The pair stood in anticipation of the return but what they eventually saw was not what they were expecting. Whilst the dust plume got bigger and bigger on the horizon, they both turned to look at each other and Susan Brown pointed her arm to the right, indicating that Maria Da Silva had ventured off in that direction and therefore it was unlikely that the plume was being made by her convoy. As the red cloud got larger it was evident that it was being made by something else, as there was a morphing of light material which was constantly changing shape, with an occasional thin arm extending from either side of the frightening swirling vision.

"Phillipe, what is wrong?" was heard inside his helmet, as Mission Control had identified from his suit crystal that his medical condition was becoming unstable.

"There is something strange on the horizon!" was his reply, and he switched on his suit camera to affect a transfer of the information back to Earth.

"Phillipe, get back into Mariner Twenty."

There was no need for Phillipe to speak any more and he tugged at Susan Brown's left arm and hurried them both back to the air lock. The pair scrambled up the stairs and into the relative safety of the capsule and they quickly started the procedure of closing the outer door. Their hearts were racing at a level that had not been seen before; not even at the initial launch, nor when landing.

The air lock procedure seemed to take an eternity but eventually the pair were faced with the surprised look of Juan Cortez, who had been engrossed in his fourth game of chess with the on-board computer. He was rather unceremoniously pushed out of the way as the harassed pair fought for a sight of the apparition through the appropriate facing window.

"Did you see that?!" exclaimed Susan, to an even more puzzled Juan.

"See what?" was the obvious reply from someone who had been in his own world.

"That! That thing!" and she pointed at the window.

"What thing?" was all that Juan could say.

"Okay let's calm down. Whatever it was has gone now" said Phillipe in a semi-controlled voice.

Their discussion was interrupted by Mission Control:

"Guys, calm down. All of your vital signs are too high. We'll look at the video and see what we can analyse."

Unfortunately, the intended calming tones of Mission Control were interrupted by the brightest of lights filling the cabin with an intensity not witnessed by them before. The trio belatedly shielded their eyes from the glare and as the light subsided, they were further catapulted into fear as a loud 'bang' shook Mariner Twenty.

"We're under attack from that thing!" screamed Susan Brown, who by now had truly forgotten everything she had been taught about stress management. Her blue eyes took on a fearful expression as the shock remained within every fibre of her body.

The three huddled together, as if their lives were about to be taken from them, with the normally very restrained Phillipe Bertrand also being compromised by the mini hysteria that Susan was emitting. As the oldest crew member, he normally conveyed a calming image of statesman-like stature, with pleasing mid-blond hair and green eyes, but even he was joining in with the destructive atmosphere. Again, Mission Control tried to calm the situation:

"Guys, you are safer inside the craft. But where are Maria, Anna and Jon?"

In their own fight for survival they had lost sight of the fact that they were only half a crew.

"They're not back yet. We thought that thing was them returning but they had set off in the opposite direction," responded Phillipe, as Susan systematically viewed the vista from each of the capsule's four windows.

"There's nothing there," were meant to be the comforting words from Susan, but deep down her fears were that something was hiding and ready to attack again, and even though her short cut mousey hair was welded to her skull with the sweat of fear, she nevertheless felt as though every strand was standing erect in anticipation of a further bombardment of her senses.

Meanwhile another member of Mission Control had contacted Maria Da Silva via the crystal communication system that was embedded in her suit. The information was passed onto the frightened trio with the news that they were safe.

"Okay guys, Maria, Anna and Jon are safe. They had some trouble with one of the pods, which must have landed on the side of a ridge, as it has rolled down and they have been trying to extract it. They are on their way back. We've told them what you've experienced. They saw the flash and heard the noise too, so we had to tell them that it wasn't an explosion of our making. They'll be back soon. Now can we all calm down until we actually know what has happened? We're investigating the data now."

"Okay," was said in unison.

"Juan can you give the team a once-over? We can see that the levels have dropped but nobody appears to be relaxed at all."

"Sure," replied Juan Cortez, who was secretly glad that he was finally being called into action.

In the confusion nobody realised that the two quads had returned, having aborted their attempt to retrieve the damaged pod. The air lock was soon being used again and all six were reunited.

CHAPTER SEVEN
Don't Reveal

The next press conference was due and this time Roger Haines and his panel were expecting a rougher series of questions. Computer Room 6 had been busy the previous day, filtering the live feeds so that those on Earth only saw what they were allowed to see. Consequently, the conversations about what had been seen and heard, were still locked away and a more restful set of images had been portrayed to whoever had been watching. But as ever, there is always somebody who notices something odd and the conspiracy theories start doing the rounds.

It should have been no surprise when the opening question from the representative of the French news outlet, *La Monde*, opened the batting with a corker. Speaking into his phone in French he asked the following:

"Mr Haines, we noticed yesterday that there was a potential loop feed of Phillipe Bertrand and Susan Brown when they were outside the craft investigating the contents of the pods. I assume the live feed was stopped for some reason and we were fed a previously seen series of images instead. What was the reason for this?"

Roger Haines tried to hide his distain of the Frenchman,

who had been an aggravated soul whenever he was present at previous press conferences. At the pre-launch, the launch and the intervening journey, he had always found a question that tried to undermine the project. The answer was off the cuff, as Roger Haines himself had not been aware of this particular scenario, but he felt best placed to try and answer before any of his panel colleagues volunteered an alternative.

"Thank you, sir," responded Roger Haines, not wishing to acknowledge his foe by name, before continuing:

"The system often uses a loop link when we have a problem with a feed from any of the static cameras. If there is an interruption to a feed, rather than show you a blank screen, which itself would encourage you to question us, we just start a loop again of what is already available. I hate blank screens, don't you? We then catch up when the fault is rectified. We know that Juan was working with the on-board computer during his spell inside Mariner Twenty; we think he may have knocked a switch that temporarily cut the link."

'La Monde man' smiled in satisfaction that he had made Roger Haines slightly uncomfortable. His follow up question was also a beauty:

"Mr Haines, thank you for your version of the situation. Can I further ask you what Juan must have switched on, or off, accidentally at 3:26 yesterday, when you can clearly see that something mysteriously moves mid-video feed? A writing implement is static on the console and then it is a couple of centimetres away…do you know why? Was he experimenting with teleportation?"

This had Roger Haines truly beaten and he had no alternative but to concede defeat and volunteer to investigate on his foe's behalf.

"I don't know. I'll investigate and come back to you at the next press conference. Now where is Philip Jones from *Sky News*?" responded Roger Haines, trying to move away from 'La Monde man' and onto someone hopefully more supportive and less inquisitive. Philip Jones stood up in the front row taking Roger Haines by surprise.

"Roger, we were informed that Maria Da Silva returned with Anna and Jon without a pod. Why was that?"

"Philip, thanks for your question. The pod that Maria tried to retrieve had actually rolled down a ridge and was embedded in a pile of Martian dust. It became too difficult to manoeuvre the thing in the time available, and so they will try and retrieve that one on another day, probably starting first thing in the morning. Unfortunately, it was carrying the sleeping quarters and bathroom gear, so the crew aren't happy about that!"

There was a collective giggle from those in the auditorium.

"Thanks Roger. So, when do you think the crew will have the pods in their required formation and how long will that take?"

"Philip, I am not sure how difficult the retrieval of the living quarters pod will be. All I can say is, once all the pods are back at Red Base, then it is a matter of moving them into the two 'X' positions and cutting through both connecting arms, then sealing the intersections with the crossways that are inside one of the pods. In practice on Earth, in conditions as near as we could make them to what they are experiencing, it took two days to do so. If we can get it done in that time, I would be very pleased…Right, Sen Patel from *India Today*. Go ahead please."

Sen made himself visible at the right-hand side of the

seated area.

"Mr Haines, why is there nobody from the Asian Continent in the crew?"

Roger Haines didn't have to think long before replying, as he was pretty sure that he had been asked a similar question about two years previously.

"Sen, thanks for your question. We did consider all sorts of potential candidates but as you know, India does have its own space program, as does China, and we were reluctant to steal their best people and be accused of thereby pushing their own missions back. We have Anna Ling, who whilst born in America, does have recent ancestry in Malaysia, but we couldn't fill Mariner Twenty with somebody from every nation. Maybe on subsequent trips we will ask those governments if they would be willing to provide some personnel."

"Thank you, Mr Haines. Do we know what has been retrieved so far?"

Roger Haines smiled at another easy question.

"Sure, Phillipe and Susan did the stock take and they have enough bits and bobs to survive. The remaining pods do contain valuable merchandise but the food production and recycling equipment are in situ, together with a couple of science pods. Now, if the pod that had to be aborted is not complete enough, then we will have to make a decision as to what to configure differently. It is likely that if we are one pod down then we may dispense with the quad storage facility."

The press conference continued with the questions not necessarily getting any harder, and after the required time had been exhausted, Roger Haines closed the meeting, realising that his companions on the panel had been surplus to requirements;

he had hogged the whole experience.

He felt obliged to climb the stairs again, to enquire of the mystical team in Computer Room 6 as to what he should do about answering 'La Monde man's' awkward question. He consequently approached the door with a degree of anticipation as to what story would be deliverable. The twin entry process was carried out and Roger Haines again found himself in the inner sanctum. He wasted no time in approaching his youthful grey-haired friend.

"How are we going to answer that question about the pen moving? I didn't know anything about that."

The grey-haired figure had already swiveled his chair around to face him, but instead of answering the question, invited Roger to approach one of the screens on his desk. He made a few clicks and an image appeared in front of them. It was the footage from Phillipe Bertrand's suit cam. It only lasted a few seconds but it was evident there was something within the vortex of red dust that defied explanation.

The image continued to play on a loop and on each play the image repeated its journey. The red cloud had something in it that moved erratically. It would morph from one unknown shape to another with a thin wavering arm occasionally breaking free from either side. The image played again until the grey-haired man stopped the process and turned to confront Roger.

"What do you think that was?"

"I've got no damned idea! What is that?!" replied a startled Roger Haines.

The grey-haired man volunteered the only option he could think of:

"It could be another life form; a shape-shifting life form. Whatever it is, it looks angry. We've enhanced the footage as best we can, but we can only come up with an alien life form that looks like nothing we have on Earth. That's not all, your French guy was correct. There is something else. The crew think they were attacked by it."

The grey-haired man pressed another button and played the footage from inside the cabin. The picture showed the three crew members in an agitated state, repeating the fear of what they had seen. The whole screen then went a brilliant white, and about two seconds passed before the image returned to a more normal state of sharpness, but then was interrupted by a loud bang. The crew could be seen huddling together in a mixture of shock and fear.

"That's why the pen moved. Either the crew nudged the console and the pen got dislodged, or the shockwave of sound shook the cabin enough to make the pen move."

Roger looked at his friend, with a face that nobody had seen before.

"Why am I only seeing this now? Why wasn't I shown this yesterday?!"

The grey-haired man calmly replied:

"I can't show you this sort of thing before we have tried to provide an answer, and anyway, we have the toughest job holding this back and putting something else on the screen for the viewers to look at. Maria's team saw the flash but didn't see it directly. They heard the bang too, and we had to tell them that it wasn't Mariner Twenty exploding, but we have a theory about what it was. Take a look at this."

The pair again returned their attention to the screen and

a further few buttons were pressed. This time two images were on a split screen showing a view from two of the external cameras mounted on Mariner Twenty. One was trained on where Phillipe and Susan had been working and the other was declaring an image at right angles, and merely looking at a view of the horizon. The glare on the first screen followed a similar pattern to the image of the craft interior; an image of bright light that subsided after about two seconds, but which also indicated that the light source was moving away from the craft. The second image confirmed this theory, as whilst the source could not be seen directly, the resultant bright image allowed some of the screen to present a picture of a travelling light source. Both cameras then juddered as a shock wave of sound permeated the technology.

"It's a meteorite!" exclaimed Roger Haines.

"Not quite. Your nemesis said that at 3:26 the images showed that the pen had moved. We plotted the courses of the orbiting rockets used to deliver the pods to Mars. The rocket that delivered pod three was due to pass over that general area at 3:25. We haven't been able to pick up its signal again. It's pod three's rocket that crashed through the Martian atmosphere and created that problem, probably because somehow it was on a lower trajectory than the others. That's the solution."

Roger smiled.

"So that's half the problem solved, but can we discount that the alien fired something that brought down the rocket, and that it is trying to warn off our crew. And what about that alien thing itself?"

"I think there's only one solution that will have to be done shortly; we'll have to get Maria to send out drone eleven or twelve to investigate. We are going to have to be careful. If there is some form of life out there, we are going to have to tread carefully and think like they would. How would we react if some alien life form landed on Earth? That's the problem."

CHAPTER EIGHT
Meeting the Alien

Whilst the majority of the crew were away on a journey to try and retrieve the stricken living quarters pod, Jon and Maria remained back at Red Base. Jon had been tasked with preparing a revised plan for the eventual survival pod's layout should the total number be reduced to a useable eight containers. It was a simple enough task for the engineer, but there was a need to delay his final solution as he had to consider the implications of a ninth of their solar panel array being defunct. Meanwhile Maria Da Silva stated that she was going outside with one of the camera drones.

The crew had felt considerably better now that the flash, bang, wallop experience had been nothing more than a pod rocket crashing down, and somehow the fear of an alien attack diminished as the crew began to realise that there was possibly a genuine explanation for the strange creature seen on the horizon. The fear had gone but curiosity reigned.

Once outside, Maria held the camera drone aloft with her right hand. Whereas the smaller drones relied on automation to lock onto the nearest available VHF signal, the camera drones were piloted by the crew member. This was achieved by matching the camera drone to Maria's bio signature, and by her moving her arm and hand in unison to signal to the drone what it should do. By raising her arm, she would instruct the drone to rise into the air, and a flexing of her fingers to the fully outstretched position would advance the drone in whichever direction her arm was pointing. A tilt of her hand, either left or right, would tilt the drone accordingly, and by clenching her fist would instruct the drone to stop and hover.

The corresponding picture feed was projected onto the inside of her visor and as usual she would see the actual image about half a metre in front of her. For this reason, she had to remain static, as she would be blind to whatever was actually around her, such was the detail of the image she would be receiving.

The drone shot off in the general direction of where Phillipe and Susan had last seen the alien form. As it sped across the Martian landscape, the camera picked up the detail of the surface with rocks and boulders coming into view at regular intervals. The drone was soon at the ridge, behind which it was assumed there would be some kind of markings in the Martian soil. There was nothing immediately evident and consequently Maria sent the drone higher so that she could get a wider view of the landscape. As the drone climbed higher, a larger and larger portion of the ground came into view, all of it with an orange hue that bordered on being red.

There appeared to be the remnants of a tornado track on the ground, as there were a series of spiral patterns etched into the soil. This presumably was what had threatened the crew, but this was just what was left as evidence of the existence of something rather than the actual alien itself. Maria waved the drone further away, following what she thought was the reverse progress of the object, hoping to find perhaps a cave or crack in the Martian surface that would have provided an opportunity for a lair. Unfortunately, her exploration was cut short as the drone was now too far away to receive her instructions, and so an auto-stop feature kicked in and it hovered in a stationary position whilst awaiting the next order.

Maria had no option but to trace the tracks back towards her, and so she moved her arm and fingers in the appropriate manner and the drone retraced its route back to where it had first picked up the trail. Maria then sent it along the remaining portion of the track.

The drone was operating at a height of approximately one hundred metres and it was now on the horizon ridge. The track seemed to follow along the hidden back of the elongated mound.

After a travel of about five hundred metres something came into view in front of Maria. There was a distorted light object of no particular shape, which she guessed was partly covered by Martian dust. It was large in total area but had no specific form. This must be what the crew had seen, and what they had been so frightened of, but was it dead, resting, or setting a trap for her? Her heart began to pound, so much that her concentration was interrupted by Mission Control asking her if she was okay.

"Yes, don't worry, I think I've found something."

"Roger. Be careful," was the reply.

Maria Da Silva invited the drone to edge lower towards the sleeping giant, and with each reduction in height came the corresponding increase in her heartbeat. The image in front of her provided more and more detail. She was now about fifty metres above the alien who had still not stirred. She was half expecting the thing to leap up from the ground and grab the drone, giving Maria the first look inside an alien's digestive system, but nothing happened.

She edged the drone lower; she was now forty metres above her target. Lower still, until at twenty metres she stopped, again waiting for the alien to attack; but still nothing. Perhaps it was asleep, or maybe even dead. Instead of hovering in a static position, she moved the drone around, and on each movement, she still had no idea what was going to happen. She lowered the drone further whilst surveying a larger area of the alien in closer detail. Now she was actually so low that the hover blades caused a slight downdraft and moved some of the red camouflage that the alien had covered itself with. Finally, she had something to shout about:

"Stupid, silly bastards!" she blurted out.

"What?!" replied an astonished Mission Control.

"I said stupid, silly bastards!" repeated Maria Da Silva, who by now was laughing uncontrollably.

Mission Control remained silent, not sure what to say or do next before finally interrupting Maria Da Silva at a point in her mid-laughter:

"Can you update please?"

Maria composed herself, and in-between what were now giggles, she finally described what she was seeing.

"It's a damned pod chute! It's a parachute from one of the pods that was released on landing. I can see the 'HAINES' logo on it! It must have got picked up by a Martian twister. I cannot wait until I show Phillipe and Susan! What idiots!"

"Okay, okay. Return the drone to Red Base and have your fun later."

Still giggling, Maria instructed the camera drone to return to her and as it sped back, she got an ever-closer picture of herself. Even with her spacesuit on, the drone picture being relayed back onto her visor could not hide the fact that she was giggling as her shape twitched. She caught the drone with her right hand and positioned it into the 'off' position. She laughed again before climbing up the external steps and back into the air lock.

Her smile said it all and Jon was forced into asking why she was so happy, as he was expecting her to inform him that they would have to abort and leave the planet as she had seen the alien and been threatened.

"What did you find?" was the natural request.

"A pod parachute! They saw a pod parachute that had been whipped up by a Martian twister! I'm going to have fun with this!" responded Maria, who was now desperate for her colleagues to return.

Luckily, she didn't have long to wait as a plume of red dust outside the window indicated that the jokers had returned. They carefully lowered the damaged pod onto the ground. Whilst the sides seemed intact and undamaged, the solar-panelled roof now held a series of cracks which formed a confusing pattern of lines reminiscent of the London Underground map. Hopefully it was just the glass that was damaged rather than the cells, but that would have to be a job for Jon Lightly to conclude.

Maria Da Silva was hoping that the new convoy crew would get out of the quads and she could laugh loudly at them, but with the pod collection not complete, she felt the disappointment as the two quads set off to continue the quest.

"Oh," she remarked to Jon, "my fun will have to wait."

As there would be a good hour before the crew would return, Maria suggested that Jon take a quick look at the new pod and give his opinion as to what the damage was. Jon agreed and proceeded to put on his external suit. Maria checked the connections and he was soon outside and detailing the damage. Maria was now alone in Mariner Twenty and it gave Mission Control the chance to inform her of the next Martian mystery that needed to be solved.

"Maria, MC here."

"High MC," responded Maria.

"Look, we have another mystery for you to solve, which we want you to keep from the rest of the crew."

"Okay," said a surprised Maria.

"You'll remember that drone ten took a looped route back to you, and we all thought that it had aborted a possible collision with drone one that was on its return journey?"

"Yes," said a hesitant Maria.

"…well, it did latch onto something. There is a tenth piece of something out there that's emitting a signal. The signal was weak but there was definitely an echo that drone ten locked onto. We need you to investigate. Unfortunately, it's too far away to rely on a camera drone so you'll have to get nearer to it. We suggest you take one of the quads out for a drive in that general direction and then release the camera drone from there. If the crew can be kept busy planning and putting the pods together then you can probably carry out the task without anybody really noticing."

"Okay, but what do you think it is?"

"Well, I know we've had a lot of false alien stuff recently, so I'm sure that there is a good and simple explanation, but we don't want to speculate at this stage."

Maria thought for a moment before concluding:

"Okay, so hopefully the boys and girls are retrieving the final pod now and so tomorrow they can set about putting everything together. I'll say that I'm going for an explore in one of the quads, just to make sure that there's not a better location for us to try; something like that, maybe."

"Roger that," was the confirmation from Mission Control.

Maria Da Silva sat down slowly on one of the console-facing seats and stared out of the window at Jon, who was now making his way back to the air lock. His demeanour suggested a problem and so she awaited the inevitable bad news, which seemed to enter the main cabin before Jon himself.

"Solar panels are knackered. They're only producing about 25% output. I may be able to patch it up a bit but we won't get much more out of them. Probably means that we'll have to leave anything on charge for considerably longer than planned. I suggest we swap the original quad pod with this one and only charge up one of the quads at a time. We can then have the living quarters in a fully functioning pod. Luckily the kit inside is pretty much okay so we should have comfy beds at last."

"Okay," replied Maria, with a look of disappointment on her face that was hard to disguise. "I suggest that we charge up the quads tonight using the intended pod and then rearrange everything tomorrow. Is there anything else that may have compromised our mission?"

Jon Lightly looked back at his Commander and held an expression of doubt in his face.

"We don't know what the other panels are like. I'm banking on them being sound enough for at least 80% efficiency, if it's much lower than that, then we could be constantly behind on the mission schedule."

Maria mirrored his expression but with a bit more concern resting in her mind. She wanted to be remembered, not only as the first person to set foot on Mars, but also as the commander of a successful mission. To be recalled as a failure would be too depressing for her, not that she would be meeting members of the public who could ridicule her, and so she quickly dismissed that thought and got on with preparing herself for her clandestine mission of the following day.

CHAPTER NINE
Reveal the Conceal

The familiar '6' appeared on Roger Haines's phone, requesting him to take the short journey to the room that effectively controlled the Mariner Twenty mission. He entered the sealed room using the usual practice of a double electronic lock release.

"Hi," he said, as he approached the bank of desks.

"Morning," responded the sender of the message, "take a seat."

Roger pulled an adjacent chair nearer to his companion, as if they were going to whisper secrets to each other.

"I expect you'll be delighted to know that we have solved two of the three mysteries."

"Yes, most definitely," replied an expectant Roger Haines.

"Okay, so we won't know about the rogue pod ten until we get Maria to send out the camera drone, so that mystery remains, but seeing as nobody knows about that, then they won't be worried about it either. The 'flash & bang' was the demise of pod rocket three and that has been confirmed by the signal terminating too, so that just leaves us with the mysterious alien. It was a chute that was picked up by a Martian twister; it was something from Earth not Mars."

"Phew!" said a very relieved Roger Haines. "Okay, so what do I say to the press?"

His mysterious friend surprised him by suggesting that he actually convey the truth to them.

"You can start by responding to 'La Monde man' and tell him that the demise of pod rocket three caused a temporary blinding of our cameras, and because of the confusion, the pen got jolted from its original resting place. The pod rocket signal ended at that time and that can be verified by any of the other space agencies. Say that we didn't want to reveal that until we were certain of the reason. I don't think you need to mention the alien incident at all, but if somehow somebody hears about that, again we can tell them the truth; it was one of our own parachutes caught up in a Martian twister. We're not telling any lies and it also deflects away from what is still a mystery; what is giving us a signal from that rogue pod. Again, nobody should know about that. That should satisfy everybody."

Having concluded their meeting, Roger Haines set off for his daily interrogation in the adjacent hall. As usual the room was full and in expectant mood, as if awaiting the answer to 'La Monde man's' curved ball. Roger Haines approached the steps leading up to the platform where his team were already sitting. He smiled in the general direction of the floor but without expectation that it was destined for anybody in particular. He sat down in his usual central position.

"Okay, before we start, we had a question from the floor from *La Monde* that asked about the moving pen…"

There was a hushed silence rather than a uniform giggle that Roger Haines had been anticipating. *Tough crowd today,* he thought.

"…well we didn't want to tell you at the time, as we needed to check our facts, but the incident was the result of a quasi-meteorite that crashed into the Martian atmosphere nearby. The result was that we lost a couple of seconds of footage due to the shock waves, and one of the crew consequently nudged the console on which the pen was resting. Now, before you ask – because I don't want anyone to waste one of their valuable questions – the meteorite was in fact the rocket used to supply the team with survival pod three. For some reason it was on a lower circling orbit of Mars, and after three years or so, it finally entered the lower reaches and resulted in the meteorite-like experience for the crew. As you can imagine, it shook them up a bit but they are all okay now."

Roger Haines tried to locate his foe in the crowd, as if to get some acknowledgement or approval, but he wasn't visible.

"Let's move on; Luis Gonzalez from *CATV*".

"Hello," said an excited member of the audience who was located on one of the right-hand edges of the seating area.

"Can I ask you a wider question about the technology being used, please? I understand that there is zero delay between the two halves of the crystal communication systems, and that there is no way that any transmission between the two can be intercepted, but can we just get clarification as to what back-up systems are in situ if one half of the crystal is damaged, as I understand that the system is then useless."

Roger looked along the table and volunteered his communication expert to step up to the plate. Susie Letts was again called into action.

"Luis, you are correct that if one half of the crystal is compromised then that pair of crystals, and whatever it is embedded in, becomes inoperative. So apart from the crystals in the Mariner Twenty craft itself, we have separate crystal systems in each of the crew's suits. There is also one in the orbiting rocket that delivered them to Mars, which we can use to monitor a few functions, and also one embedded in a small printer that is on-board Mariner Twenty. Then we have a traditional back-up VHF system in each of the craft, and again in each of the crew's suits. In addition, each pod has a VHF system embedded in it, as do the two quad bikes. The drones have a VHF system in them too. But any VHF signal currently takes about fourteen minutes to get to us here at Mission Control, and it would take a similar time for any response back to them, so any conversation using that medium would take about half an hour per exchange. We are therefore only using that in an emergency, although the crew will be able to talk to each-other using VHF quite easily."

Luis nodded in acceptance and proceeded with his second question:

"Could you explain to me how we see the crew entering the main cabin in clean suits but when they enter the airlock from outside, they always appear to have a thin film of red dust covering them?"

Roger Haines nodded for his tech expert to answer. Today that was Hero Kuchin.

"Luis, we have two problems with the 'ins' and 'outs' of the crew. The first is the dust that you alluded to. If we have too much of that entering the cabin, then that can get into every little crack that we don't know about and eventually potentially compromise parts of the operation. The second aspect, which is probably even more important, is that we don't know what microbes they could be bringing into the craft that could have a devastating effect on their health. So, you may have noticed that when we have a camera view of the air lock, there is interference on the picture. This is because either the air lock is being opened, or because the extraction process is taking place. The extraction process involves a rapid exit of air and a corresponding blasting of neutralising particles, which are known to kill any microbes that we know about, so we hit them twice and hopefully that does the job. We think we have everything covered; previous robotic probes have analysed the soil and they didn't find anything out of the ordinary, so we are just being extra careful."

Hero smiled at his questioner, indicating that he had completed his answer. Roger Haines took the signal and volunteered the next questioner to make himself known:

"Bob Stokes from the *BBC*…go ahead Bob."

"Roger, we know that one of the pods is now damaged. Could you give us an update on that situation?"

"Yes Bob. The pod itself is intact and okay. It didn't hit any rocks or boulders as it rolled down the slope, and so the interior stuff is okay as far as we know. The problem is with the roof and the solar panels. Jon Lightly, the engineer, has had a look and he thinks that they are only about 20-25% working. His task will be to try and get some repaired and increase the output, but we are going to be a long way from the near 100% that we planned on. So, the likely outcome is that they will swap this pod, which was to be the living quarters, with the pod that houses the quads, and use the damaged pod to house those instead. What does that mean? Well, effectively that the charging of the quads will have to be done one at a time and will probably take twice as long for each to be re-charged to full capacity. It will be an inconvenience and may slow the team down a bit but at least those panels aren't totally gone."

"Thanks," said Bob, who followed up with:

"So, noting that there is a lot of dust floating around that seems to settle on everything, and that the crew are going to be down on available power, how are they going to maximise on the generation if there is a constant film covering the solar panels?"

Roger again jumped to the answer.

"You may recall an answer from the other day when somebody asked about the usefulness of the drones, which were assumed to only have one purpose; that being to locate the pods. They can be bolted to a frame and used to carry small items – or even a crew member – but the added function could be to hover over the panels and blow the dust off. They may have to do it each day but it should solve the problem…*CNN*, Steve are you out there?"

Steve made his location known and joked whether he should use the auto translate facility as he was from the Deep South. Giggles all round, even from those in the audience who didn't understand the inference.

"Roger, the cost of this project…couldn't the money be spent more wisely on alleviating the suffering back on Earth?"

"Steve, as always a searching question!" said Roger, realising that 'La Monde man' had an accomplice.

"It's like this, at some point we are going to have to leave the Earth and look for a new home for mankind. Now, whether that is because of war or famine, or asteroid impact, or pandemic disease; who knows what will be the final catalyst, but all I do know is that the sooner we establish viable colonies elsewhere, the sooner we will be able to ensure that the human race has a chance of existing into the future. Put it this way, if I spent the five trillion dollars this is costing on trying to eradicate starvation on Earth, what if a pandemic disease then wipes out all those fit people, or a war kills us all off? That five trillion dollars is gone and we will be stuck on Earth with no means to escape the carnage; you see?"

The questioner then followed up with the obvious next question:

"So, who decides who gets to be saved on this new world; people with the money, I assume?"

Roger again felt obliged to tackle the questioner:

"Steve, don't worry we won't be asking you to make the journey; we're not planning that far ahead!"

There was again a collective giggle from the audience as the inference was that Steve was too old even now to make such a journey. After waiting for the murmur to die down Roger Haines continued:

"Look, the primary objective is to get talented people up on Mars who can start a new civilization. That is probably decades away and anything other than a small village is all we can hope for at this stage. By the time humankind has got to the point where it can send humans up there in large numbers, who knows what the criteria will be."

Steve sat down thinking he had achieved something.

"Lola Pertria from *Euronews*, are you out there?" continued Roger Haines, hoping to move away from the subject. Lola stood to attention and asked her first question:

"The ESA is apparently ahead of schedule with a joint

project with Haines Inc., involving in-flight production of spare parts using the large format 3D printers that the ESA had developed a couple of years ago, but I understand that you are holding back on sending the equipment up to Mars. Is there a reason for the delay?"

Roger Haines again took control of the situation.

"Lola, we could send the pod unit up tomorrow given the favourable weather forecast, but the trouble is that the distance between Mars and Earth is now quite large. We would be better off hanging on until the two orbits are nearer together to ensure a shorter journey time. In addition, until we know exactly what the crew are actually in need of, we may have to delay the 3D printer delivery and send a different cargo up instead; maybe food production or something we haven't even thought about as being required."

Lola looked slightly embarrassed as her desire to push Roger Haines into a corner was countered by her lack of knowledge of the positioning of Mars and the Earth. She nevertheless continued with question two:

"The small 3D printer on board Mariner Twenty can presumably be used for small format parts, such as latches and electrical connector coverings, and I appreciate that there is a small supply of plastic material on-board too. Likewise, in the large format 3D printer pod there will be a supply of raw plastic and a robotic arm to deliver it to the business end of the operation, but what is the technology that will provide a raw material when the plastic is exhausted?"

Hero Kuchin was probably best placed to volunteer a response.

"Lola, that's a very interesting question. The answer is why we chose to send three scientists up on the first mission. They have first-hand experience of using natural material to make replacement artificial substances. Consequently, the numerous bits of scientific kit that we sent ahead of them will allow them to use the Martian soil to manufacture all sorts of things, from something resembling concrete to quasi-plastic components. They will also be able to extract the water content from the soil, to split into oxygen and hydrogen, and from there we have the possibility of drinking material and fuel. There is a lot of kit up there that can hopefully do wondrous things. Now, the larger 3D printers will be able to produce the bigger parts that may be needed. I believe they have a near two metre maximum dimension facility, so they could be used to repair panels on the quads, or indeed probably manufacture a small additional building. We have high hopes for this."

Lola sat down, probably grateful that she wouldn't have to ask anything until her turn came around again in about a week's time.

Roger looked at his watch and declared that perhaps they should end the session there.

CHAPTER TEN
Pod Ten

Maria Da Silva looked down from the window of Mariner Twenty and surveyed the full collection of survival pods which were arranged in a reasonable formation below. Today five of the crew would be collating supplies and manoeuvring the pods into their formal planned positions. Unfortunately, Maria Da Silva would be on a mission elsewhere, hunting down the elusive pod ten, or whatever it was that the rogue drone had detected.

Whilst the original plan was for her to take one of the quads to locate the rogue signal source, both quads would be needed to fix the survival pods together. Maria would therefore have to experiment with the drone copter; a contraption that used a frame and the ten drones to lift her body. She had tested a more powerful version back on Earth, and she hoped that the reduced gravity on Mars would compensate for the weaker lifting power of the smaller drones that she now had access to. She had therefore instructed the crew to find the frame first so that her flight could be done quickly.

She had joked with Phillipe and Susan that she was off to find more aliens on the Martian landscape, but having exhausted the humour from that incident, it was now time for some serious searching and she told the crew that she was just doing a reconnaissance to get a better understanding of the area, just in case a more suitable location for a base was evident. She had no intention of moving the base but the crew didn't know that.

She was pleasantly surprised when the crew found the frame early in their search and this was acknowledged by a 'thumbs up' from both Maria and Jon, who was the finder below her. He then knew that he would be tasked with fixing the drones to the frame and bolting the lightweight seat to the underneath, which being an engineer, he achieved in a matter of minutes.

The crew were now using the VHF communication system to talk to each other; all the pods had been retrieved and there was therefore no reason for them to curtail the use of this method of communication.

Maria Da Silva requested that one of the team return to the craft so that she would be able to experiment with the new-found method of transport and carry out her hidden task of locating the rogue tenth pod. Anna Ling duly took up the request and she was soon back inside the main cabin exchanging pleasantries with her commander, who had changed into her external spacesuit and was ready to exit the enclosure.

She was met at the bottom of the stairs by Jon Lightly who had the assembled hover drone awaiting her arrival. He had tested that all the drones were working correctly and explained how the contraption worked. Basically, she would be situated in a lightweight chair that was suspended from the underneath of the frame, atop which were mounted eight of the drones. Two further drones were mounted at the back of the frame and were permanently facing backwards, and below them was a small enclosed box which housed a few tools and camera drone eleven.

The eight top drones could each tilt by approximately 90 degrees in all directions, thereby the overall effect should be that the drone could take off, hover and journey forward with ease whilst also having the ability to swerve both left and right. Due to Maria's weight, the hover drone could only manage to hover at a maximum height of about three metres, which was plenty high enough for what she assumed her task would require.

She duly strapped herself into the seat whilst the machine was stationary on the Martian soil, and placed her right gloved hand onto the joystick which was built into the right-hand side of the frame. Atop of the joystick was a button that drove the power to the drones. She tentatively pressed this and was instantly levitated up into the air at a height that cleared the nearby Jon Lightly. The machine hovered for a while, churning up an ever-increasing cloud of red fog that indicated perhaps Maria should get on her way and leave the remaining crew to work in a clearer environment. She consequently drove the hover drone away from the immediate area and practised some manoeuvres before finally setting off in the direction indicated on the inside of her visor.

She had the intensity of the image set to 25% so that the majority of her vision was concentrating on where she was going, and on the terrain of the Martian landscape that was passing beneath her. Her progress was evident by the path of red dust which followed her route, and the five crew members all looked in her direction until she was physically out of sight, although the red cloud continued long after her disappearance.

She raced across the Martian landscape; some was familiar to her but most parts were virgin territory with the odd feature that separated the interesting from the tedious. One such feature was an indentation in the soil that seemed to run for several hundred metres, as if the ground had collapsed into a void underneath. This was exciting news as there was speculation that water and other useful elements could be buried beneath the Martian landscape and this looked as though it would be a suitable access point. Either that, or it was a dried up river bed; either way it hinted at water and thereby the potential for life.

After about fifteen minutes Maria Da Silva reached a spot which indicated that she was within a camera drone's distance of the weak VHF signal. She consequently turned off the switch that drove the rotors and the hover drone slowly sank to the red floor under its own weight, assisted by the thin Martian gravity. She anticipated a sudden landing but the machine was remarkably well behaved.

She unstrapped herself and waited for the dust to settle around her before walking around to the back of the machine and taking the camera drone from the cabinet below the rear rotors. She held the camera drone aloft, which as before, was matched to her bio signature that would enable her to control the destination by the movement of her right arm and hand. The drone followed her command and set off for the intended location, with the images relayed back to the inside of Maria's visor, which she had now set to 100%.

The crystal-clear images raced before her and such was the experience that she had to slow the object down for fear of the journey being a catalyst for her falling over. She attributed this to a version of motion sickness which had been presumably exaggerated by the thinner Martian atmosphere and her fifteen-minute journey. The images slowed to a near walking pace which enabled Maria to re-equilibrium herself, and once she felt satisfied that she wasn't going to fall over, she allowed the camera drone to accelerate at a faster pace.

She knew that she was roughly in the correct area from where the rogue signal had been sent, and as she moved the drone higher into the sky, a larger vista opened up to her. In the far top corner of her visor vision was something that she thought looked out of place; a crack in the surface held something potentially non-organic in its grip. Maria slowed the camera drone and moved her arm to lower the picture frame to a more concentrated area.

The camera approached the strange object from an angle at a height of about ten metres and slowly edged downwards trying to get a better view of what appeared to be something being eaten by the Martian surface. The object was definitely not a natural occurrence. Even if she didn't know what it was, it looked as though it was unbalanced, as if part of it was trapped in the surface crack and the rest of it was at an unnatural angle. She moved the camera drone in closer; any danger that the camera drone would be attacked was negated by her curiosity. Her heart started to beat faster and this alerted Mission Control to her potential plight.

"Maria, are you okay?" requested the voice in her helmet.

"Yes MC. I think I have found something but I'm not sure what it is," replied Maria, who was still studying her find intently.

The object still did not move and as Maria instructed the

camera drone to move even lower onto the stricken shape, the draught from the rotors started to clear the area of the red dust which had obscured part of the object.

"It's one of ours, I think," said Maria, as she surveyed the clearer image of what she was now viewing.

"It looks ancient but I think it is something we may have sent up," and as the rotors cleared an ever-increasing collection of Martian dust, the truth of the mystery was revealed.

"It's the Mars Polar Lander!" she exclaimed, "when did that go missing?!"

Mission Control hesitated before volunteering a response:

"That was way back, are you sure that it is the Mars Polar Lander?"

"Yep, definitely it. I'm going to journey over to it."

And before Mission Control could dissuade her or warn her to be careful, Maria Da Silva had recalled the camera drone and was busy packing it away and strapping herself back into the hover machine that would take her to the solved mystery.

The hover drone took off, clearing the surface beneath her and enveloping her in a subsequent cloud of red fog. She sped off to the location marker that was now projected onto the inside of her visor. Luckily, the 100% image concentration had automatically reverted to a 25% mode that enabled her to actually see where she was going, and within a few minutes she was landing adjacent to the Mars Polar Lander.

She couldn't wait to leap from the copter and stride over to the metallic object. She slowly reached out her gloved hand and touched the historic craft. It was at an angle of about 30 degrees, with part of it lodged into what appeared to be a crack in the Martian surface. Maria had to be careful not to disturb the ground as she too didn't want to be trapped in her new environment. She however thought she should pay this ancient technology some respect, and brushed away what dust she could so that the craft was returned to a clean state that it should always have been.

Various bits of the craft looked out of tilt from their intended position and so Maria tried to give the craft some honour by adjusting what she could. She straightened an aerial that was impersonating a fishing rod, and wiped the solar panel, and eventually the sun reflected off of the new clean craft. She switched on her suit cam so that Mission Control could bear witness to her theory being correct.

"Yes, that is definitely it," confirmed Mission Control, "return to Red Base, please."

"Roger," responded Maria, with a voice that sounded pleased with itself.

She climbed back into the hover drone and headed back to her colleagues, leaving the ancient monument in a resplendent museum-like condition. The technology of the Mars Polar Lander had long been surpassed by decades of scientific advancement, but there was a warm feeling inside Maria at being able to touch history.

Back at Red Base the five crew members had started with the huge task of emptying some of the survival pods and connecting them in the desired pattern. The plan was to configure an initial 'X' pattern out of four of the pods with an interconnecting pre-constructed crossway, which was in four parts within one of the pods. This was engineered to form a seal where the four pods met at their open ends. One of these ends would be cut open and matched to the other 'X' formation and the two pairs would again be connected by a sealed connector.

The first four pods were connected and in situ about twenty metres away from Mariner Twenty. One end had been removed with the help of a quasi-plasma cutter. Various boxes of supplies were stacked around the project, awaiting formal stowing away in their new home, but first the remaining four pods would have to be constructed in mirror formation and connected to their twin via the main airlock connector. Then the air inside could be configured for human occupation and finally the crew could feel as if they were home.

The activity was interrupted by the sight of a red plume which announced that Maria was on the return journey. She deliberately slowed the hover drone so that it landed away from the opening of the block of pods and away from her colleagues. Having switched the rotors off, she unbelted herself and did a wave to the crew who had started to move towards her.

"It works then," confirmed Jon Lightly, perhaps looking for some acknowledgement of his handiwork.

"Yes, sure does," replied Maria, "…but guess what I found out there?"

Susan Brown and Phillipe Bertrand looked towards each other, fearing that Maria was about to say that she had found another 'parachute alien'.

"What?" they both said nervously.

"…the Mars Polar Lander! It must have crashed as it's on its side looking a bit sorry for itself."

It was evident that some of the crew weren't too knowledgeable about historic Mars missions, and so Maria tried to educate those that were in need:

"It was launched decades ago, and was one of the high percentages of craft that never made it to fruition. It's in a ditch at an angle. I don't think it ever sent back any information, and it was assumed to have crashed, which it looks as though it did, judging by its condition, but I gave it a clean-up out of respect and it's almost back to its former glory."

There was a sort of appreciation from the rest of the crew, but most of them probably thought that Maria had been out for a pleasant Sunday drive whilst they were busy trying to complete a gigantic 3D puzzle, but they were pleased for her, if not for themselves.

CHAPTER ELEVEN
The Past Meets the Present

Roger Haines again found himself sitting at the front of the stage at the next press conference. The world had new experiences to discuss and the journalistic family had been tasked with asking the important questions.

"*Fox News*; Celia Rodriguez, please," said Roger Haines, starting the proceedings.

Celia rose from the sea of anticipating faces and asked her first question:

"Roger, we finally heard from the crew themselves yesterday via their in-suit VHF communications, and I must admit that I think we all found it useful. Do I take it that you are relying on the VHF system for the crew to interact with each other and just let them get on with life, and if they need Mission Control's help, they use the crystal method?"

This was a rather simple question, which Roger looked across at Susie to answer.

"In a word 'yes'," responded Susie, "now that we have all the pods together, which we relied on the VHF signals to locate, we have no need to restrict its use, so 'yes.'"

If only all the questions were that simple to answer, but this was just the calm before the storm as question number two was thrown at the panel:

"So, are you happy that amateur radio hams back on Earth can potentially pick up these conversations and that the crew might let sensitive information out into the marketplace?"

Susie again volunteered a reply:

"In reality, we have difficulty in picking up their conversations without enhancing the quality in-house. There is solar wind, radiation and Earth's electronic interference that can all degrade the quality of the signal, and that is why we waited until we could use the split crystal system to ensure an instant speech process, and one that would not be affected by external matters. If any of the VHF conversations do make it back to the amateur community here on Earth, then we will live with that, but I doubt if the quality will be sufficient to excite anybody."

Susie smiled at Celia who mirrored her expression. Roger Haines however knew that perhaps Celia was playing a waiting game. He knew that the Mars Polar Lander had sent some form of weak VHF signal that was picked up on Mars. He hoped that it was so weak that it got absorbed into whatever other signal a radio ham may have been listening to. In reality, it would surely have just been a signal of indeterminate beeps rather than a recital of a Shakespeare play.

"So, can we have David Stern from *The Orlando Sentinel*?"

"Hi Roger," said David, in a manner that determined that he and Roger knew each other.

"Hi Dave. Good to see you."

"Likewise. You must be proud that your first discovery is finding the Mars Polar Lander that was lost on landing. Do you think there is any mileage in trying to repair it, as I understand that it is on its side?"

"Dave, that is a good question, but let's be honest, that craft was using technology that has been surpassed. I am not sure that cell phones were even in existence when that was sent to Mars, so the language that was programmed into it has probably changed, and I doubt that there is anybody alive today who would know how to understand if it said anything. But as a museum piece, should we ever build a museum up there; maybe!"

"Following on from that, we were told that the Mars Polar Lander is on its side; can you elaborate on that aspect?" continued Dave.

"Yes, Maria found it sort of embedded at an angle of about twenty-five or thirty degrees. It looks as though it is stuck in a ditch or an old river bed of some kind, although her first recollection is that it may be in a crack in the surface, which is why she didn't spend too long in the vicinity. I think she also noted a similar feature when travelling out that way, so this may be a geological feature that is common in that area."

Dave nodded in appreciation and let Roger Haines move onto the next inquisitor.

"Sebastian Lubinski, from *Nordic TV*?"

"Here, Mr. Haines." An upright hand from a seated position indicated that Sebastian was unable to stand.

"Do we know why Maria found the craft? Was she looking for it, as I believe that it was in the general area of where drone ten had flown?"

Roger Haines had been dreading this question, as he too realised that Mission Control had not censored the route that Maria took, and it was evident that the location was in the same area that drone ten had gone rogue. He felt obliged to take the question:

"To be honest, we just let Maria choose her own route whilst testing the effectiveness of the hover drone. I think she wanted to get a general idea of the area. She'll probably cover all the surrounding areas, one area at a time, over the next few days, so that she can get a good idea of the immediate terrain. There are a few ridges around them, which restrict the long-distance view that they have, so I think it's only natural for her to want to explore."

"Thank you, Mr. Haines, but you will realise that there is a coincidence that she heads in the direction of where drone ten had been, and she finds a crashed craft from an earlier era. Is that not suspicious?"

Again, Roger Haines thought he would be best placed to take the heat out of the question:

"You'll appreciate that Maria Da Silva is a highly intelligent and knowledgeable commander. I was partly responsible for getting her to apply for the position, and I know that she has a good knowledge of Martian probe history. She can reel off dates that probes were launched, what they were designed to achieve, what they discovered and when any went missing. She will know that there are probably a couple of stranded probes somewhere in the *Planum Australe*, and I suppose on one of her trips she was bound to find this one. She doubtless will find others on future days away from Red Base, but I suppose subconsciously she may have chosen that route because of what drone ten did. But I cannot answer that it was a deliberate attempt to find the Mars Polar Lander."

Roger Haines wished to curtail that line of questioning and

so quickly moved on.

"Okay, Lionel Bridges from *The Australian*."

"Here, Roger." A tall thin man stood up at the right of the hall.

"Can you elaborate on how the construction project is coming along? I think we can see that the first 'X' is almost complete, but presumably the second one will need to be bolted on and tested before the crew can finally move in."

Roger Haines looked along the panel for today's volunteer engineer. Colin Lucas was spotted at the end of the line, and the nod in his direction invited him to earn his salary for the day.

"Well Lionel, you are correct that the first part seems to be coming along fine. They didn't report having any trouble with cutting away the end of the relevant pod, and we know that this morning they also managed to put the second seal on the crossways portion of that completed unit, so fingers crossed, that bodes well for repeating the process with the second portion. Once they are complete and connected, we will have to run the pressurised test for twenty-four hours, and if there are no problems, we can then get the crew to move the kit into its required locations within the module, and then they can formally move in when they feel ready."

Lionel then asked question two:

"So, are they behind, ahead, or on target for completing the unit?"

"I'd say they were behind. It took longer to retrieve all of the pods, and one was damaged, meaning we had to swap some around. In addition, the dust is causing some irritation by getting in the way. You've seen how easy it is to disturb the soil, and it does seem to permeate where you don't want it to.

I think once they are ready to move in, we may have to have a further twenty-four-hour period where they put the filtration extraction system on to give the insides a really good clean."

"Okay people, we'll call it a day. Thanks for your interest and keep the questions coming," was Roger Haines's way of saying: 'I've had enough, now go to the bar and enjoy yourselves'.

Because of the awkwardness of some of those questions, Roger Haines felt that he should take a trip up to computer room 6 and quiz why Maria's path was conveyed to the public on a route map, when it was obvious that it would match that of drone ten. He thought that he deflected the probing query but still he felt that somebody somewhere didn't try to protect him. He approached the room with ID card in hand, which released the first electronic lock. He placed his phone against the second plate and the door in front of him opened to allow him access.

"Hi," he said, as a sort of announcement that he had arrived uninvited. The grey-haired voice was quick to interrupt what was going to be his rehearsed gripe.

"Sit down."

"Okay," said a bemused Roger Haines, as if he was in front of the headmaster for some misdemeanour.

"Yes, I know we didn't keep the commander's route off screen, but if we hadn't put something on the TV then you would have been asked even more probing questions, and anyway, there is something more mysterious that you would want to know."

Roger Haines looked in surprise at this last statement and totally forgot about his own question that he was going to ask.

"What's that?" was all he could muster.

"Right, look at this," and with those words the grey-haired voice flicked a few buttons. His computer screen removed itself from sleep mode and projected two horizontal graphs into view. They were placed one atop of the other; one red and the other green. He pressed a further button and two lines of the same corresponding colour began to dance across the screen from left to right, before repeating the journey again. They traversed across the screen for a third time before Roger Haines felt obliged to ask what he was actually looking at:

"And what does this represent?" he asked, in a manner that was both inquisitive and belittling at the same time, for he was still mildly annoyed that he hadn't got his position across. The answer was swift:

"The top green line is what we picked up originally from drone ten when it locked onto what turned out to be the Mars Polar Lander's signal. The red line underneath is what is now being picked up by the VHF receivers in the crew's helmets. We've managed to dilute it to a slight background rumble, and have told them that it's interference because they are working with so much metal around them, and therefore there is feedback, but you'll note that both graph lines are the same. I can only surmise that when Maria cleaned up the Mars Polar Lander, she has inadvertently strengthened the signal and it's now being picked up by the nearest VHF receivers, which is the crew's own systems."

"Okay, so we now assume that the Mars Polar Lander is actually active after all these years. We should be proud of that, shouldn't we?" remarked Roger Haines.

"Well yes, I suppose so. But look at the gaps and the lengths of each of those two signals."

Roger Haines squinted, as if trying to pay more attention and submitted:

"Okay, so again, what am I looking at?"

"The Mars Polar Lander was designed to send back information in presumably some form of code; binary, or whatever we were using back then. That does not appear to be a code; that looks like repetitive speech of some kind."

Roger Haines again squinted at the screen before agreeing.

"Yes, it looks like the same thing is being repeated. I suppose it could be: 'Hello, I'm here and well', but it doesn't have that feel to it. Is there any chance we can increase the strength and perhaps hear what is being said?"

Roger Haines felt that he had at last caught up with the status of the conversation between the two men and that they were now on a more equal footing, but again the grey-haired voice was ahead of him.

"I've asked Maria to turn up the VHF receiver strength in Mariner Twenty to maximum but turn the speaker volume down to zero, that way I can hopefully use the extra 'oomph' in the on-board system to bounce the Mars Polar Lander signal to us here. There will still be mild interference in their own helmets, but that will just be a slight background noise rather than something that will interfere with their ability to communicate with each other. Meanwhile we may actually be able to hear something tangible."

That all seemed rather logical and so Roger Haines had nowhere else to go with the conversation, apart from asking the obvious:

"So, when should we be able to do that?"

"Any minute now, as I asked her to carry out that task about an hour ago, so giving her time to stop what she was doing and get back into Mariner Twenty and adjust the VHF settings, we should be hearing something soon."

As if by magic, Roger Haines was reminded that there were actually three other people in the room who had always been intently staring at their screens, and who had never said anything, but now came the required words from an unknown individual:

"Patching it through to you."

The pair of conversationalists both turned back to face the computer screen. The lines continued to bounce across the screen in their familiar pattern, but now there was a matched sound; sound that didn't make any sense, but it was actual sound:

"Ego cognovi veniet…ego cognovi veniet…ego cognovi veniet…"

The phrase was repeated until the sound was muted, but everybody in the room now looked in the same direction towards the grey-haired voice and Roger Haines, as if to say: 'what the hell was that?!'

Roger Haines was first to say something:

"I'm pretty sure that NASA didn't build that into the Mars Polar Lander program. Any idea what that is? It sounds like a language of some sort."

One of the faceless, and up until now, voiceless individuals, volunteered to engage the auto-translate program which had been used in the press conferences. A few buttons were pressed and the system tried to analyse the spoken words which were again being repeated in the room. There was an unfortunate silence, which was only occasionally broken by a single word:

'come'. The word was repeated at irregular intervals, as is if the computer program was guessing at the meaning, rather than translating it from a bank of the world's major languages, and the word 'come' was the nearest that it could evaluate from a series of words that presumably meant something more detailed. The grey-haired voice offered his thoughts:

"Okay, I suppose that's a start, but it's pretty evident that whatever that is does not originate from a major Earth-based language. I thought it might be Russian, so it looks as though we are back to a definitive code that NASA was using for that mission; perhaps to deliberately stop the Russians from learning what was going on. The trouble is, I doubt that there is anybody alive today who would have worked on that mission and who could help us in deciphering this. Perhaps we should just accept that this is part of history and leave it alone."

Those were logical words that reinforced the fact that technology had moved way beyond the confines of the Mars Polar Lander. Mariner Twenty had its own mission to fulfil, so why waste time with a piece of historical twaddle? But Roger Haines wasn't so sure, for he had the faintest recollection of the basis of the words being repeated. He held his head in his hands, which were resting near his chest, and portrayed a troubled image of either a man in great pain, or in deep thought. He muttered the words into the palms of his hands:

"Ego cognovi veniet…ego cognovi veniet…"

He concentrated on the one word that was somewhere in the vaults of his educational memory: *veniet, veniet…veniet.*

"*Veniet…veni!*" he blurted out loud, returning to an upright seated position.

"*Veni…Veni, vidi,vici*…I came, I saw, I conquered! It's Latin!

NASA was using Latin to fool the Russians and that's why the computer can only recognise the word 'come', as it's probably similar in Italian!"

There was a partial recognition on some of the other faces in the room. None were apparently as knowledgeable as Roger Haines, and not one of them felt the courage to dismiss his theory. He obviously thought he knew the answer, and therefore he thought that the code had been broken. He had one word deciphered but what about the others? When strung together what was their meaning, and was it just a message to say that the Mars Polar Lander had arrived, and was it therefore awaiting a confirmatory signal from Earth? Would it just keep repeating the words until Earth acknowledged receipt?

"Can you work out the rest of the phrase?" asked his companion.

"Not immediately, but in theory we have the start of the process," replied Roger.

The grey-haired voice didn't want to dwell on this subject any longer and so felt obliged to remark that this was not their primary concern:

"Look, you continue with the Mariner Twenty project and if we get any spare time we'll try and fathom out what it all means, but let's be honest, whatever the Mars Polar Lander was designed to do has been surpassed by intervening probes, the result of which is that we have six humans on that planet. They should be our only focus."

He was of course correct, but Roger Haines felt as though he had only one last clue to complete a particularly difficult crossword, but he reluctantly gave up his quest and agreed to return to his main task.

"Okay," he said, "…but it was a bit of excitement, wasn't it?" The grey-haired voice agreed and the two parted company.

The two electronic clicks which Roger Haines instigated on his exit, told him that perhaps this day was over. He couldn't think that any future press conference would raise the question of the VHF interference but even if it did, he had the 'too many metal objects giving feedback' as a solution.

All was well.

CHAPTER TWELVE
Settlement & Unsettled

The final centre section of the survival pod structure was lifted into place by the pair of quads. There then followed a detailed inspection of all the joins, by way of a hand-held x-ray gadget and a heat source mapping program, which was projected onto the inside of the crew's visors. At this stage the crew had to confirm that the structure was sound and that it was ready for a formal pressurisation test. The test would run for a full twenty-four hours to enable the structure to adapt to a different pressure rating, and it would also detail whether any breaks in the structure were evident. The crew would therefore spend a further night in the Mariner Twenty quarters.

The pod structure had been connected to form the required two 'X' shapes, linked by a central air lock unit, with an approaching tunnel that had all been pre-formed and stowed in one of the pods. It had been tested back on Earth in various conditions, but to try and protect the structure further, one of the secondary tasks would be to manufacture some form of brickwork from the Martian soil which could either act as a windbreak, or become part of the structure itself. Each of the pods had been furnished with the required contents, so there were several scientific labs that could carry out experiments, manufacture small bits of spares and useful objects, and others would grow food and recycle waste. There was a solitary pod that was the living and sleeping quarters and another which was split between a bathroom and a kitchen.

There was artificial light in all the pods, but each central manufactured portion that connected the four arms of the individual 'X' shapes was transparent, and so this afforded a reasonable degree of natural light, albeit with a red hue. Atop of each of these connectors was the extraction system, which also had the added benefit of being able to pressurise the immediate area if the main unit failed. With two of these units atop of the connecting areas at either end, this would be a decent back-up system. And of course, the crew could always use Mariner Twenty in an emergency.

Each of the eight pods had a roof with solar panels, which would manufacture the power for all of the crew's activities, but as the crew highlighted earlier, these would have to be kept clear of Martian dust if they were to work efficiently, and so the hover drone was likely to be called into action on a daily basis. Storage was spread along the length of the two interconnecting arms of the 'X' structures, thus limiting the width, but being central, most of the supplies were easily accessible.

In addition to the main structure, the additional damaged ninth pod stood away from the main complex and housed the two quads, that would have to be charged separately due to the reduction in power that the damaged solar panels would be providing. The hover drone was also squeezed into the same unit, and all could be kept relatively clean by being shut away behind the front door flap.

Having completed their epic construction project, the crew

retreated to the relative homely Mariner Twenty for potentially one last night of sleep. There was an air of anticipation as Jon Lightly remained outside and programmed the pressurisation unit to carry out its task. There was a slight whirring followed by an encouraging sound of something more substantial happening as the unit sprang into life. His fearful side was expecting the transparent walls of the entry and connecting points to flex inwards, followed by their total collapse and an inrushing of Martian red dust, sucked in by the over strength mechanism, but his happy side was victorious as the unit remained totally rigid. He banged the side of the entry point as if congratulating his handiwork. All was well.

And when everything is going well there is only one direction that will follow. Luckily for the Mariner Twenty crew, they were not going to experience the problem; Roger Haines was. He and his team had just finished the day's press conference, which had gone smoothly with nobody asking any searching questions that would put him on the spot. The questions were all based around the construction of the pod complex and the wellbeing of the crew, and so Roger Haines had exited the meeting feeling as though the day was going to be an easy one. He was in two minds whether to take the stairs up to his mysterious colleagues but didn't want to interrupt them if he had nothing to say. The press conference went well and so he decided to head off to his rest quarters for the remainder of the day.

His temporary home was an individual single storey unit that was housed within the grounds of the Mission Control complex. There were about twenty such dwellings, all designed to be used by the senior positions on the Mariner Twenty project, and which also afforded the individuals the chance to rest without an arduous drive to a formal residence many kilometres away. The individuals would also be on call should something go wrong overnight, or whilst they were generally resting.

His house was a functional abode rather than a glamorous one. It had everything he needed and being a multi-roomed unit he could have friends and relations to stay, but he had forgone that benefit as he needed 'cave days' where he could be alone to reflect upon the project and future missions.

His immediate thought was when he should send up the next pod rocket and what should be in it. If everything went well, he had the large format 3D printers already packaged, but he really had to wait a week to ensure that the Mariner Twenty crew had everything they needed. There was nothing to stop Haines Inc. from sending up several rockets a few days apart; the rockets were already built, but the main issue was trying to ensure that the distance between the two planets was as small as viable. It wouldn't be as small a distance as when Mariner Twenty first departed the Earth, but he should be really taking advantage of the current momentum of the project. Thereafter, any supply mission could take twice as long to reach Red Base.

The walk to his house was about ten minutes and along the way he would cross paths with fellow workers with whom he would exchange brief nods of mutual appreciation. Nobody stopped him for a chat, as there was an unwritten code that suggested if a person was in the vicinity of the housing zone, then they were off duty and therefore not readily approachable. This worked well and defined the respect that everybody had for each other. Except that today he was stopped. The man that approached him was his grey-haired colleague from computer room 6.

At first Roger Haines didn't really recognise the man as they had always met in the darkened surroundings of the mysterious room, and here he was in glorious technicolour, the sunlight bouncing off of his blue shirt and dark grey jeans. He had eyes too; blue eyes like his own.

"Hi," he said, with an element of surprise in his voice that he couldn't disguise or mute.

"Hello Roger," replied the grey-haired voice, which somehow sounded friendlier outside of the Mission Control building, as if the sunlight and the open air diffused the otherwise official tone that he had always heard.

"What's the problem?" enquired Roger, with a natural curiosity.

"Can we talk in private; your house, maybe?" was all he got as an initial answer.

"Okay, mine's probably nearer," responded Roger, nodding in the general direction of his house, and the two men briskly walked towards the salmon pink building which was his temporary home. He waived his ID card in front of the electronic plate that unlocked with a satisfying click, and they were soon inside a relatively cool open-planned interior.

"Same design as mine," said his colleague, which surprised Roger as he thought he had the superior model on the estate.

"Oh," he replied nervously, "…drink?"

"Sure, I'll have a beer with you."

Roger moved over to the kitchen area and opened the fridge to retrieve a pair of brown glass bottles.

"Glass?" he enquired.

"I'll take it as it comes."

Roger duly pinged off the caps using a wall mounted opener, which was designed around a condensed map of the Solar System; relegated Pluto had been replaced by the opening that facilitated the bottle-top removal. He strode over to his friend who had availed himself of a seat on one of the two sofas that faced each other.

"Here you go," he said, taking up position opposite his visitor, "so, what do you need to tell me?"

The visitor took a swig of beer before declaring his opening position:

"You recall the message we got from the Mars Polar Lander, and that you recognised one of the potential words…?"

"Yes," interjected Roger.

"Well, we managed to get the rest of the transmission analysed, and translated it equates to: 'I knew you would come', which doesn't sound like something NASA would build into its mission."

"No, it doesn't. Are you sure that is what it means?" was the inquisitive response from a perplexed Roger Haines.

"Yep, we've had a government department go through it."

"Why would you involve the government in this?" was an even more inquisitive response from the host.

His visitor took another swig from the bottle before declaring a further card in his hand:

"Look, I know I am on the payroll but I need to be honest with you, as I think I owe it to someone who has spent most of his adult life planning, and eventually sending, a successful mission to Mars. I was placed here by our government to ensure that the mission went off without any nasty surprises. I know this is a private project, but as a US citizen the government needs to ensure that its people aren't getting out of step with expected policy. That is why we have the two-minute delay, so that anything that is seen that shouldn't be seen can be edited out, and I'm not talking about the public being spared the sight of the crew exploding when they depressurise because of an accident. There is the possibility of alien life on Mars that the public should be shielded from. If we have a little green man suddenly pop up in the camera view, what do you think that would do to the population back on Earth? I'm not sure that they would be ready for that."

"So, where are you going with this?" enquired a now slightly angry Roger Haines, who was beginning to think that a little green man had been seen on the screens in room 6.

"Once we knew what was being said we decided to reply with a suitable Latin phrase, as we anticipated that we potentially could start a dialogue. Initially we didn't know whether we had just awoken the Mars Polar Lander, which would then start sending back information, but it transpired that we were able to have a conversation. We could ask it questions."

And with those words the visitor placed his phone on the table in front of them both and played the message:

"Etiam hic sumus"

He continued:

"Basically, we were acknowledging the message and after about half an hour we got a further, different message."

"Non tutum, globe nobis non est tutum."

"We had established alien contact. We had a first encounter; something that we had always hoped for but which we were equally scared of, as we didn't know where the journey would take us. Would we eventually be wiped out by their superiority, or would we wipe them out because we have something natural in our world that would eradicate them? Should we ignore them altogether and just plough our own furrow?"

Roger Haines interjected:

"What did they say?"

His visitor took a further drink from the bottle, this time emptying it.

"Our world is not safe," and he gazed into Roger's face and saw the look of puzzlement and horror in equal measure staring back at him.

Roger didn't say anything but headed back to Pluto and the fridge to prepare two more beers. He turned around and gingerly walked back to the sofas; his confident stride had gone.

"So how is our world unsafe, and do they mean Earth or does 'our world' mean Mars, where they presumably are? Which world are they talking about?"

His visitor again took a large gulp from his newly arrived replacement.

"I can't say anymore but I have been requested by our government for you to accelerate the departure of the next series of rocket pods…and to keep building them as quickly as you can. There can be some hidden funding to assist with any pinch points you may have. And we need you to build more human transport facilities; bring those to the fore of your plans too."

Roger Haines took a larger than normal slug of beer from his bottle.

"You're planning an escape mission; an exodus, but we haven't got detailed plans that far ahead which would build anything more than a small village. There will be billions of people left behind!"

His visitor was now holding an empty bottle but his throat was lubricated enough to continue with minimal information:

"We don't expect you to transport all of humanity to Mars. We just need the safety net of Mars to hopefully allow the human race to survive, should the worst happen and these prophecies hold truth."

"You know considerably more, don't you?" responded Roger.

The embarrassed visitor sighed and replied as best he could whilst diverting away from the question:

"I don't think I can stress how high level this scenario is. I can tell you that next week, the highest of high-level people in each of the countries that have space programs, will be brought into this realm. Each of them will be planning with urgency to get their missions underway. The public will know nothing. They will be fed the line that so successful is Mariner Twenty, that they can now send their own people to Mars."

"So, it will be a space race."

"Probably an Olympics of space races," replied the visitor, getting up from his seated position, retrieving his phone and heading towards the door. He had final words to declare to his host:

"You realise that you will not be saying any of this to anybody else; nobody. And in addition, we have had to block your access to computer room 6. We can't have you diverted from your intended mission by getting involved in a different dialogue. Once the crew are permanently installed in Red Base and they vacate Mariner Twenty, I will get Maria to tweak the craft's VHF receiver so that any distortion is minimised. We've not picked up anything in the chatter rooms about this yet. If you need assistance, you have the number in your phone and I can direct you if you get any sticky questions from the press. Just accelerate the mission. Oh, and if you need any encouragement in this situation, think of all the crystal communication systems you'll be providing to the other space agencies."

The two shook hands before they parted and Roger Haines found himself alone, which was always his intention, but he was alone with one huge secret that he somehow had to keep hidden. He remained behind the closed front door, transfixed by the sofas that had witnessed the news. His visitor walked away from the house, held his phone up to his face and pressed a pre-programmed number. It produced a short dialing tone before clearing to a silence, inviting him to speak.

"I think he'll be on-board. I think he should be invited."

All was not well.

CHAPTER THIRTEEN
Protect & Survive

The following day's press conference had been delayed by a couple of hours so that the results of the pressurisation test could be concluded and analysed. The system had been checked for a full twenty-four hours and now the crew could switch on the extraction equipment to ensure that the interior was as clean as it could be. In a couple of hours, the Mariner Twenty crew would be the formal start of Red Base.

Roger Haines again sat in the centre of the long table at the front of the stage. The normal array of inquisitive faces was staring back at him, awaiting him formally starting the proceedings. He was excited that things were going well but also perturbed at the news he had been given the day before. He just hoped that nobody had bugged his house and the world now knew about a potential alien encounter.

"Okay, let's see who's first. Collette Muset from *Die Welt*; go ahead."

Collette had made herself visible even before addressing the stage; her bright yellow dress and matching jacket was a rare glimpse of colour in a sea of dark suits.

"Can the panel tell us whether there were any problems with the overnight pressure test, and when do we consider that the crew will formally abandon the Mariner Twenty craft and start living in the pod complex?"

Roger responded whilst looking along his short line of colleagues for a volunteer to answer:

"I'm not sure if that counts as your two questions but Bob, would you like to take that one?"

Bob Rogerston took the baton. It was evident that whilst Roger Haines was a permanent fixture on the panel, the remaining team would rotate. Bob hadn't been seen before and he consequently took full advantage of his slot.

"Thank you, Collette. We didn't have any issues with the pressure test and the extraction system also performed to the standards set, and so the crew should be good to go during the remainder of the day. There isn't much for them to move from Mariner Twenty to the pod complex, apart from some sleeping gear and a few bits and bobs, so give it a couple of hours and they should be finally ensconced in their new home. I would stress that we are not shutting down Mariner Twenty and it will remain available to them should the need arise, and there is a problem with some aspect of the air system in the pod complex etc."

"Thanks Bob," said Roger Haines, ending his colleague's speech as he didn't want any negativity creeping into the discussion. His gaze was again drawn to the sunflower amongst the dirt:

"Go on Collette have another go!"

"Thank you, Mr Haines," replied a grateful Collette. "What are the first jobs that the crew will be doing?"

Bob again was invited to respond to the question.

"Well, although it's a small complex it has many different

separate sections and so I suppose the group should familiarise themselves with where everything is. Although we have the main science section down one end, we also have another science pod in the other 'X' where the sleeping quarters and personal sections are. The stores are in the connecting corridor, and although it's all been marked, I still think that the crew should know exactly where the spare 'this' or 'that' is kept. They've also got to set up the camera system, as presently we can't see inside the pods; we only have external shots from Mariner Twenty, so that should be the first job. After that, we will be leaving it up to Maria and her crew to decide whether they want a good rest, but I expect that the science guys will be itching to start experimenting and developing stuff, particularly the recycling system."

Collette nodded in acceptance and drooped down to a resting position.

"Ling Losi, from *China Today*?" said an inquisitive Roger Haines, looking for another brightly dressed individual. Disappointingly, Ling was one of the dark dressed people which morphed into the rest of the crowd, but her shout of 'here' from the back soon adjusted Roger's gaze to the rear of the hall.

"What will the crew be growing in Red Base?"

Roger Haines this time invited another newbie to share their knowledge and Bill Constable was the chosen one. Bill cleared his throat before volunteering an answer:

"Ling, the seeds sent up will need to be nurtured, and until the team have inspected and studied them for a few days we will not know whether they will take or not. The plants that are already formed, and were growing in transit, tend to be high protein beans and shoots that don't take up too much space, but there are also various herbs. One of the continuing comments from previous astronauts was the blandness of the food and the unattractive nature of its presentation, so we thought that some fresh herbs would add some welcome Earth-based familiarity to their taste buds. They will also be growing some hybrid protein-based foods and also baking their own bread. I know that last one may be a bit of a surprise but there is something about fresh bread; the smell, the taste, the texture, will all be appreciated, I'm sure. There is no meat on this trip, apart from dry-packaged stuff, but we will not be rearing cattle up there!"

Ling smiled before asking her second question:

"What about liquids?"

"Well Ling, there is a small amount of water that the crew had with them, but going forward they will be using extraction from soil and condensation collection from a specialised piece of kit. Then they have some maps of where we think frozen water may be hidden underground and in permanently shadowed craters. And don't forget there will be a good percentage of liquid in the food they are eating. But I take your point; water is extremely important now and going forward."

"Thanks Ling," interjected Roger Haines, "…okay, Sudit Rahm from *Space Today*."

One of the dark jackets stood up from the middle of the hall.

"Thank you, Mr Haines. Where is Mission Control with future journeys to Mars? I know the other day you were awaiting the progress of this Mariner Twenty project, but do we now have any timescales for future trips?"

Roger Haines thought that he should take this question, particularly after his unplanned discussion with his grey-haired friend yesterday.

"I think that so far we are happy with what has happened and therefore we will be announcing some future dates, probably in the next few weeks, unless the progress of the Mariner Twenty dips."

"And what if it does dip, what are the plans then?" was the follow up question.

"Well, it depends where the dip is. We have the large format 3D printers ready to launch but if there is a problem with say, the food production equipment, and they have to manage with only one functioning system, then we would probably send up a replacement bit of that kit instead. It just depends where any problem is – but we're not anticipating any problems!"

There was a slight nervous giggle around the room.

"I think we have time for one more delegate; *Euronews*; Simone Verity."

Simone stood from within the ranks.

"I think we heard somewhere that Maria Da Silva has access to a stun gun. Is that really a necessary item to take to Mars?"

"Gosh! That's a bit of an odd question!" remarked Roger Haines, who consequently took the question himself.

"Well Simone, we don't know whether all the calm attributes, which the crew displayed during their year-long training on Earth, will continue to be at the same level in the confined environment that they now find themselves in. We don't anticipate any trouble between the crew but if there were to be, it was considered wise to have some form of secondary control mechanism, apart from the standard hierarchy of commander and crew. So as an extreme safety measure we thought that Maria should have some additional means of maintaining authority. It can't kill anybody; it's just a mild stun gun."

"Thank you, Mr Haines," declared Simone, with a smile before continuing:

"Is there any plan to send up some form of robotic humanoid figures to assist with routine tasks and heavy stuff?"

"Not at this stage," answered Roger Haines, "when we get to the stage of actually identifying a potential site – maybe underground – that may need a bit more strength in hazardous conditions, then that would be the opportune moment to send some controllable multi-function droids. We have the quads with lifting gear, but anything underground may need something more adaptable."

There was an appreciative nod from Simone and consequently Roger Haines wound up the press conference for that day.

CHAPTER FOURTEEN
Finality

The room was stark with minimal adornments. It was functional beige in colour and reasonably restful. There was a solitary map of the world positioned on one of the longest walls and a large TV screen at the other end. There was a single door that allowed access, and an array of overhead lighting which compensated for the absence of any windows that would otherwise produce natural light.

In the centre of the room was an elongated table, around which fourteen chairs had been positioned at equal distances from each other. In the centre of the table was an elaborate metallic box with fins displayed at various angles; it could have been a centre-piece art statement. The chairs were occupied by a collection of men and women of different nationalities. Some were in impressive uniforms and others had arrived in more casual attire. Roger Haines was one of the occupants and he was dressed in his standard linen jacket, tee shirt and jeans.

There was a general murmuring that wasn't loud enough to fill the room, and consequently it was relatively easy to overhear some of what was being said. Language was no barrier. The room was fitted with the indispensable auto-translate device that instantly picked up what was being said by inbuilt microphones in the centre-piece, and then conveyed to a speaker, which was somehow manufactured into the table top in front of each of the delegates. Only a very discrete series of small holes in the table top allowed the occupant to be aware of the technology.

To a casual observer, the mystery was how the system knew what language to project to which occupant, but this was relatively easy to solve; the occupant just had to say something for the centre-piece to analyse and translate appropriately. This was achieved when each of the delegates first arrived and they were given a small place card, which had already been printed with a series of words in the native tongue of the holder. Consequently, the English phrase: 'All's well that ends well' had been translated into the various languages of the delegates, and once this was stored in the centre-piece, a normal conversation could be held. Of course, the one flaw in the system was if delegates changed their location but only Roger Haines had that mischievous thought.

He didn't recognise any of the other invitees; they weren't heads of states, presidents or prime ministers. They weren't famous people from sporting environments or artists or musicians; they were just people that you wouldn't realise were important enough to be present. In fact, Roger Haines himself was the only person who could walk the streets and be interrupted by a gaggle of the public who all knew him from the infamous Mariner Twenty mission. And that was why he was present at this meeting; he had knowledge of space travel that he assumed would be vital to the potential exodus of humanity that the grey-haired voice had warned him about.

It was his slim frame that had approached him a week ago

with an invite to this gathering. It was worded rather oddly. It wasn't a threat but Roger Haines got the distinct impression that if he didn't attend voluntarily, he would be likely kidnapped and shipped by an unmarked private jet to the location. As it was, Roger Haines was in no mood to argue as he now felt that his mission was to try and save the human race from whatever it was that threatened it so drastically. There was a degree of finality to what the threat was and that was something that he felt he should try and overcome.

His personal thoughts were interrupted by one of the delegates standing to announce that the meeting was now about to start. The speaker was American and Roger assumed that he must be connected to his grey-haired colleague. The built-in speaker in front of him remained silent as there was no need to translate what was being said, but he could hear the faintest of speech being emitted from some of the other speakers. It wasn't overpowering and therefore didn't interrupt any thought process; it was just like a background rumble of noise that hardly registered. The standing man then continued with the process:

"Thank you for coming today. You probably all know Roger Haines, President of Haines Inc. who successfully put a small colony on Mars. He has been invited today to hopefully help us solve a monumental problem which we will have at some point in the future. I am not intending to go around the room with introductions as I know that some of you would prefer your identities to remain unknown. I appreciate that and will honour that request, but seeing as you all know who Roger Haines is already, I saw no harm in highlighting his presence."

There was a group nod of acknowledgement in Roger

Haines's direction, which he smiled back at in appreciation. The man continued:

"Okay, so you want to know why you are here and what could be so drastic that it requires the presence of the top space minds from around the globe, so let me start by playing you some audio. I won't get the auto-translate system to change the language, because when it was first heard the system hadn't been programmed with a wide enough range of languages, and so we had to translate using a manual method. I suppose I want you to be as confused as we were."

The centre-piece awoke:

"*Ego cognovi veniet…globe nobis non est tutum…quod ultimum…et obstretricante foraminis…oportet te relinquo… oportet te relinquere habere plures superstes vitae casus.*"

The assembled experts looked at each other and one of the delegates volunteered his knowledge:

"Is that Latin? '*Obstreticante*', isn't that obstetrics?"

The auto-translate system kicked in, leaving the Latin word intact, but re-arranging the speaker's native French into English for Roger Haines and those other English-speaking attendees, and into whatever other languages were required for the remainder of the seated individuals. The standing man volunteered further information:

"It is Latin, all of it is Latin."

"Where did it come from?" interrupted the Frenchman.

The reply was held back for a second longer than a normal conversation would entail:

"It came from Mars."

There was an audible gasp that was matched to a group expression of puzzlement. The Frenchman again took up the baton:

"So how do you know that it came from Mars and that somebody wasn't hacking into the communication channel here on Earth?"

The reply was prepared and delivered with a degree of expertise:

"We have tracked the source using a variety of methods and we know that it is originating on Mars. We are using the Mariner Twenty VHF system to collect the message, and the inbuilt crystal communication technology to bounce the words back to Earth."

"So, what if it is the crew having a joke with us all?" replied the Frenchman, with a tone in his voice that implied that he didn't want to be wrong.

The reply was passive in its tone so as to diffuse what was becoming a potential destabilising aspect to a meeting that had only just started:

"Firstly, none of the crew can speak nor understand Latin. Secondly, we have traced the origins of the signal to the once-lost Mars Polar Lander that NASA launched many decades ago. And before you ask, it is not something that NASA built into their program. The Mars Polar Lander is being used as a conduit to communicate with us."

This took the Frenchman by surprise but to maintain his momentum he asked the obvious question:

"So, what are they saying?"

Again, the reply was pre-loaded into the self-styled chairman:

"If you want the literal translation, as best as we can manage, it's:- 'I knew you would come', 'our globe is not safe', 'extreme danger', 'the birthing hole', 'you must leave' and 'you must leave to have a chance of survival'. They're all pretty drastic statements. You were right about the obstetrics, although we had no idea what that meant until we asked."

"So, you're communicating both ways and it's not just you listening to what is being broadcast?!" was the natural response from the questioner, who by now was moving away from attack mode and into curiosity.

"Yes, we have a dialogue with whatever, or whoever is up there, but it's quite a long-winded process as we initially had the problem of the time delay between the two planets using conventional VHF technology, but also that when night falls on Mars, the power on the Mars Polar Lander dies pretty soon afterwards. Now that we are beaming their messages back using the Mariner Twenty crystal communication system, we have a more instant conversation. Somehow, they are using NASA's historic mission to communicate with us here on Earth, although in reality their target audience is probably the crew of Mariner Twenty. It's a bit disjointed, almost as if they have to think before replying, but it is a two-way process."

From across the other side of the table the heavily overdressed frame of an assumed Chinese delegate provided the next question:

"So, the Mariner Twenty crew are aware of this and have they been asked to make formal contact?"

"No, they are not aware. We had them turn down the volume on their Mariner Twenty VHF system and turn the sensitivity up, so that the message is eventually beamed back to Earth and we send a reply back via the same route. They had a slight bit of interference in their helmets but we got them to dial that down a bit, so it's nothing they can really hear. As for a formal contact, I don't think any of us are ready for that. We have no idea how the crew would react to the news, let alone meeting something from another world. As such, we think it would be best to arrange for some form of Earth delegation to be sent to cover off that aspect; some people with diplomatic skills but who are also trained in a particular field that the Mariner Twenty project may need. People who are dual purpose, I suppose. We would need people who would be recognised as experienced scientists or biologists to the public but who also had a hidden talent in negotiating. Or people who had dealt with lost Amazonian tribes; people who would have a chance of being accepted by an unknown alien species. Also, we don't want to mistakenly fall into a trap, whereby they want to use our spacecraft to escape from Mars, which is a slight possibility. To be honest, the other bits of knowledge that we have gleaned can't distinguish whether the Earth is in danger or whether we are being asked to leave Mars because the danger is there."

Another delegate spoke taking up the Chinese delegate's questioning:

"So, are we here to formulate a plan to get everybody off of Mars, or are we here to send more people away from Earth? I appreciate that you suggest that the next people may be diplomats but after that, is this an escape mission from Mars or from Earth?"

"We want you all to accelerate your plans to get missions to Mars, taking as many useful people and equipment that it is feasible to carry. This is both a short-term and long-term project where we will have to work together in exchanging expertise. You will also need to look at developing rockets that can travel for longer distances, and support crews for a longer duration, as the gap between Mars and Earth widens."

At this point the chairman glanced in the direction of the Chinese delegate, inviting him to confirm what the US Government already knew. The delegate took the bait and responded:

"We have the rocket technology, but we will have to forgo our other work to facilitate this and concentrate all our efforts in the direction we are talking about here. But why should we? How do I know that this is not a trick by the world to interfere with the Chinese desire to explore space at our own momentum?"

The next words were rehearsed, to be injected into the meeting at an appropriate point, or not mentioned at all if things were going well.

"You recall earlier that I said we didn't know what the birthing hole was? Let me play you this."

"Planeta Iovis est parturientis…Iovis est rufus macula."

Again, the Latin words remained in their original form as the assembled experts looked at each other trying to decipher the message. 'Planet' was the only word that the English-speaking delegates could recognise. After a couple of minutes, and before anybody's exasperation took hold, the chairman volunteered the information:

"Jupiter is the birthing planet…Jupiter's red spot is the birthing hole. Ladies and gentlemen, the red spot of Jupiter, which has fascinated scientists ever since they could see it, is responsible for giving birth to something that is potentially life threatening to the human race. Any ideas what?"

At this point the gaze was directed towards the two women

in the room who had congregated together, presumably out of a sense of safety in numbers in a meeting where they were outnumbered by the male members. The outdated implication was that, as women, they would know about giving birth. One took the hint and responded directly in English:

"Are we talking about an ejection of material that is either radioactive, or maybe a meteor of some description?"

"Almost," replied the host, before continuing, "Jupiter has the red spot birthing hole for most of the celestial bodies in our Solar System. It is a 'planet factory', which every so often ejects a rocky object out into the vacuum of space. Jupiter has likely given birth over billions of years to all the rocky planets and moons in our Solar System."

"Rubbish!" was heard in English, but was muttered in unison by a large percentage of the delegates in numerous languages. Roger Haines listened, not quite understanding how the English word 'rubbish', which consisted of two syllables, could be represented by a collection of possibly up to eight syllables in other languages.

"That goes against all scientific knowledge," was translated through the centre-piece from an unknown speaker as the murmuring died down. "Yes," was the confirmation from somebody else.

The host remained calm before questioning his audience:

"How many times has the scientific community stated, without hesitation, that something works in a particular way before somebody else a decade later declares that is wrong, and that whatever it is, works in a different way – and that theory then becomes the truth? You may genuinely believe that the Earth was formed from the coalescence of dust and rock particles over billions of years, and which eventually formed our planet. And that another planet banged into the Earth and the remnants formed the Moon, but how can you be one hundred percent sure that is the historic case? Just because the theory fits, doesn't mean that it is the correct theory."

"But how do we know that this ridiculous theory is correct?" asked a new delegate, who may have felt obliged to join the discussion at this late stage.

"Because the thing we have been communicating with on Mars witnessed the birth of a celestial object from the red spot of Jupiter… and also witnessed the devastating results of that event."

"This sounds like a very bad science fiction novel to me," interjected another, up until now quiet delegate.

"Let me just run this program for you, which we have constructed from the hours of information that we have gathered."

With those words, the centre-piece revealed a hidden secret as beams of coloured light rose from the metallic fins to provide a revolving holographic image. All the assembled delegates could now focus on a dramatic light show.

The image showed the Solar System with all the major planets in their rough positions. The image then magnified the immediate portion that showed Mars, Earth and the Moon, and relegated the outer gas planets to out of view. The image withdrew to allow the orbits of both planets to be plotted and then withdrew further to include the position of Jupiter. Roger Haines noticed that something wasn't quite right but he couldn't be sure what the flaw was with the rather impressive light display.

The images continued to tell their story, and eventually as the red spot of Jupiter rotated into view, the ejection of a spherical object joined the collection of known planets. The ejection wasn't dramatic, like a bullet from a rifle, but rather like a gentle easing away from the red spot; a birth. The visuals then declared a line emitting from Jupiter, which gradually transferred its image to what was akin to a shockwave, and this slowly travelled across the void between Jupiter, the new planet, Mars and the Earth.

The new celestial object was small, smaller than Mars, which itself was smaller than the Earth, and it became the first object to be hit by the line representing the shockwave. The new planet waivered and it became evident that the newly born object was about to be destroyed by its own mother, as if part of a Greek tragedy. It slowly began to unravel, and the object slowly disintegrated into a collection of small rocks, which gradually spread out in a semi-circular pattern around an assumed Sun that was out of the visual field.

The image then rewound slightly and the hologram now focused purely on the approaching shockwave as it journeyed towards Mars. There was no break-up of the red mass, or a wobble that would indicate some form of structural failure, but instead there was the image of what was assumed to be the outer layer of the Martian atmosphere. It was being dragged away and into the vacuum of space. The horror continued, and this time the image pulled away to reveal a wider shot of the inner Solar System.

At this point Roger Haines realised the initial flaw, which he had noticed earlier, was that the asteroid belt had been missing; it was now there, being formed from the debris of the newly created planet.

Again, the image rewound and it now concentrated on the Earth and the approaching shockwave, which had slowed but was still going to make contact with the Earth-like image, which again didn't look right to Roger Haines. The Continents were there but all slightly different in shape and location.

The wave hit and this time the image was more detailed. The first action was that the image portrayed the North and South Poles switching their allegiances, which in turn altered the angle of tilt by about a degree; the equator moved accordingly so that it remained at ninety degrees to the new north/south line. This was followed by a graphic of the tectonic plates all shifting with a greater degree of latitude than their normal positions allowed. A series of consequential earthquakes and volcanoes erupted, tsunamis raced across oceans, and cloud cover darkened and deepened from the issuing volumes of smoke. All the known volcanoes erupted, but now those hidden beneath the Antarctic also blossomed into existence, melting the majority of the ice and effectively raising the sea level by tens of metres across the world. The Continents totally lost their shape and had now been reduced to odd pieces of land which held no resemblance to what the delegates knew today. Nearly everything that had existed was now either underwater or encased in volcanic material, which hardened to form a rocky outcrop as if nothing had been there before. The images stopped and the light show collapsed back into the fins in the centre-piece on the table. There was silence.

"So, this is what will happen?" said the nervous Frenchman, but any one of the assembled could have asked the question.

"Possibly..." said the host, who was still standing and

declaring his knowledge superiority.

"…that was what we think happened a long time ago in the distant past."

"And you have gathered that from your conversations with the aliens on Mars; how do they know that happened?" continued the Frenchman.

"Because they witnessed it," was the retort, which further silenced the delegates, "…let me continue the program."

The centre-piece again swirled into life, projecting an image of the Earth in its devastated form. The lightshow continued as gradually the blanket of volcanic fog fell to the surface and the image of the remaining landmasses became clearer. The sea receded from its peak level and more land became visible as the blue mass gave up some of its possessions. There then followed a brightening of the planet as the majority of the northern hemisphere became engulfed in a massive sheet of reflective ice and Antarctica reclaimed its natural form. The Earth wobbled and tilted back towards the correct angle and the northern ice sheet finally retreated. The continents of today became apparent as the image reached its conclusion and stopped. Instead of the programmed lights retreating into the centre-piece fins, the image just hovered above the table, slowly rotating at the required angle. The Earth had recovered.

"We are back at today," declared the chairman.

"So, if we are at today, why do we need to rush into an exodus from the Earth to Mars?" inquired the Chinese delegate.

The upright man paused before answering the question, as this was the unpalatable truth:

"The North and South poles are known to switch positions every 500,000 to 900,000 years. We never understood why, we just knew that historically over the Earth's life it had happened many times. You've all seen what happens when that occurs and we think that Jupiter ejecting a celestial object is what causes the switch. We are at the timeline when that is overdue. Our Martian friends are probably correct in that Jupiter is, as they christened it, the birthing planet, responsible for the collection of rocky outcrops that is our Solar System. Now, if you want to dilute the danger that exists when Jupiter gives birth, let me offer you this slight glimmer of comfort; firstly, what if the red spot of Jupiter is facing away from Earth when it ejects the next planetary body? What if the object is smaller than a planet and becomes a moon instead? And what if Earth and Jupiter are hidden from each other because of the Sun being in-between both planets? In all those three scenarios we anticipate that the effect will be either minimal or not even noticeable. But are we willing to gamble with humanity's existence on the basis that one of those three events are what happens next? We need to ensure that Mars is a safety net for the human race."

The centre-piece was still projecting the Earth's revolving image and therefore the next question was from somebody hidden by the lightshow.

"In the first projection it shows both Mars and the Earth being drastically affected by the shockwave. Is there not an equal danger that both could be devastated again, and both our communities will be wiped out?"

That was an easy question to answer and the obvious was forthcoming:

"Mars is the only other planet that we have a chance of colonising and we have to take the opinion that one of the two would survive. If we don't – and we do nothing – then the chances are that humanity will be extinguished. Nobody will ever know that we had a plan which we didn't bother to develop. It all depends on the orbits of the three planets at the point that Jupiter gives birth. The orbital planes are all in the same horizontal zone, but Mars takes about two years to orbit the Sun and Jupiter about twelve years, so the chances are that Jupiter will be in direct sight of either Earth or Mars for most of the future. But it might not be in direct sight of both. And of course, it probably depends on whether the red spot is facing towards or away from either planet. Now the good news is also the bad news; the Jovian day is only ten hours long so the benefit is that if the red spot is facing Earth or Mars, it quickly moves away. Conversely, the danger reappears sooner than we would like. The speed of rotation of Jupiter also implies that any ejection will have a curved course rather than a straight, bullet like journey. Again, that could be good or bad news."

"We therefore have to do this," continued the hidden voice.

"Basically, yes…and soon. We've been analysing the red spot for decades. As you probably know, not only does it revolve with the planet but it's also not a constant size; the average size of the red spot is approximately thirty per cent larger than the Earth. It's getting smaller. Again, this could be good or bad news. If it continues to shrink, does this mean that it is dying and will not be giving birth again, or is it flexing and preparing to eject another planet? Think of when you exhale a large amount of air; you position your lips into a small circular position before blowing the air out. The physics could be the same when Jupiter is about to give birth."

That seemed to get a degree of consensus from the delegates around the table as the potential horror of what would likely happen permeated their fibre. Another hidden voice from the other side of the desk stepped up to the plate:

"We need to get moving on this. How do we start the process?"

This was the positive stance that the host had been awaiting. It was all very well putting a thesis to the audience; it was a victory to get them to accept it, and a potential Noble Prize to get them to action it. The further dialogue was therefore met without much hindrance.

"First, we need to ascertain the number of space craft that we can accumulate from around the delegates sat at this table, whether they are cargo carrying, astronaut carrying or capable of both functions. Then we need to know how near to a launch date they are, and how many are in production and available for launch within the next two years. Do we have enough trained people who could manage a probable two-year journey to Mars, and then have the right psychology to survive on another planet for the rest of their lives? Do we have the necessary equipment to send them that would ensure their survival? That is your job to discuss and collate, and ultimately produce. I would also mention that our intention should not be to send high-ranking officials and state heads to Mars; we need useful people not vain career climbers."

That should have got a laugh but maybe it didn't translate properly. He continued:

"What would be of real significance is if we can enlarge whatever terraforming solutions we have. There may be enough gases present on Mars that could accommodate a partial recalibration of the planet, and personally, I think the best way forward would be to utilise what we think could be an extensive network of underground lava tubes, seal them off and develop a subterranean civilisation. Part of the Mariner Twenty project is to use the soil and extract the water molecules that are trapped within it. Then they can explore beneath the surface and hopefully find some form of frozen water that would change the whole dynamics of the project. Then we have real hope of a sustainable civilisation up there. So, I need you all to volunteer what you can provide and how far advanced you are in the various projects."

There was a slight pause before the Chinese delegate declared that their larger, long-distance rockets should perhaps be used for when Mars and Earth were further apart, rather than waste their extra distance attributes on shorter journeys. There was a degree of logic to this but also a degree of scepticism, as whilst the rest of the space agencies would be using up all their facilities, the Chinese could hold back and dictate what should happen before they sent their much larger fleet. Nevertheless, it was something that was agreed by the rest of the assembled delegates.

The Frenchman volunteered that they were advanced in large format 3D printers, and were working on a small terraforming contraption which could possibly work but it was untested. There was also a nod towards Roger Haines who already had a pod with two of the printing machines ready to go.

"We can launch that within the next month," he volunteered, "we also have a further couple of rockets ready to go; we just need to decide what to put in the additional pods. I would think food production equipment and analytical kit, but to be honest I'd prefer the crew to bed in first and let us know what they need before finalising the contents. The associated robotics with the 3D printers can manufacture on route if needs be. So, with luck, if they need something specific, it can arrive already made."

The room now started to bubble with information and ideas and the original suspicious gathering started to work together on devising a plan. Mariner Twenty-One, Twenty-Two and Twenty-Three would be launched first over the next two months, followed by the ESA missions which would send the untested terraforming equipment. Even if the thing didn't work properly, any subsequent diagnosis would hopefully provide a required solution that could either be manufactured on site or sent, albeit that it wouldn't arrive for a couple of years, but nobody dwelled on that possibility, so positive was the atmosphere in the room.

The other private space companies would concentrate on adapting their spacecraft to carry human cargo. Probably no more than four people at a time could be accommodated, but in addition they would investigate sending live embryos that could be regenerated when the technology to resurrect them followed on later missions. This would be a quasi-seed bank that would hopefully be an insurance policy should physical face-to-face breeding on Mars be somehow corrupted by the environment.

The Russian delegate, who had been relatively quiet until now, suggested that his team had been working on building an ISS-type laboratory, and that they had been planning to put it into orbit around the Moon. This was to be considerably bigger than the previous ISS and would house numerous scientific equipment that would be used to analyse material brought back from the Moon by various small shuttle craft. Their view was that several of the materials on the Moon could be mined to facilitate further exploration of the Solar System. There was an admission that this would be too complicated to build and store in a Martian orbit, but perhaps some of the rare elements found on the Moon, which they were hoping to exploit, could be sent onto Mars for better use. In particular, Helium-3 could be indispensable in providing a clean source of power and potential future propulsion material.

As each person volunteered what they could provide, the grin on Roger Haines's face grew slightly wider. The further these agencies ventured away from Earth, the more they would need to rely on his crystal communication system, otherwise the delay in the transferring of data would be just too great to facilitate a successful mission. Here was a captive audience of people who would desperately need his product.

The major plus point in his ownership of the crystals was just that; he owned the crystals. It wasn't as though somebody could steal the plans for a new communication system and replicate them; the asset was a physical item in very limited supply that only he held. The technology required to use them was simple but without the crystals the human advance would be very slow. However, it was all very well using the crystals to communicate over large distances of the Solar System, but once a piece of equipment – such as the 3D printers – which had been manufacturing on route, arrived on Mars, only Mission Control back on Earth could operate them. He would therefore have to consider letting spare sets of crystals go on a trip to Mars, which the relevant crews could use to replace the crystals already embedded in such equipment. But for the time being he would ignore that potential medium-term situation and hope that everybody would be happy with Earth manufacturing to order for their Martian counterparts.

His own current experiment was building the crystals into plants, so that a hybrid could be produced whose growth could be accelerated on Earth and instantly replicated on Mars, where it was anticipated that germination and production might be slower, or need some form of encouragement. This too would be an extremely valuable use of Roger Haines's crystal technology.

CHAPTER FIFTEEN
A Waste of Time

When the room had emptied, and the delegates were on their way back to their respective labs armed with their part of a monumental global plan, the door to the room opened and the body that was paired with the grey-haired voice entered the confines of the now quiet surroundings. He glanced at the host who had deliberately stayed behind awaiting his colleague's approach.

"They're on-board?" he questioned.

"They seem to be. It was easier than I thought. Nobody questioned where the alien was from. I think that potential subject was overtaken by the graphical display of what might happen to the Earth. I have to admit it is pretty compelling stuff to be absorbed; quite horrific really."

"At what point do you think they'll realise that it may be a waste of time?" enquired the grey-haired voice.

"Probably not for another three years or so, by which time somebody up there will go hunting for the alien colony. If they can locate the Mars Polar Lander, which should be easy enough as the location is known, then they can trace any signal back to whatever is sending it. And then they'll eventually discover that the aliens died out several hundred thousand years ago...

but at least they had the charitable nature to store all of their knowledge on some form of automated communication device which would be useful to the next visitors to Mars."

"And then…?"

"Not sure, but I hope that today we just accelerated humankind's exploration of the Solar System, because if we don't start with Mars and use that as a base to leave the Solar System altogether, then humankind will be forever stuck in the repetitive cycle of germination, progression, destruction and repeat. Do you know that the latest conversation hypothesis is that we may be the 4th incarnation of the human lifecycle on Earth? They reckon they were the third and that each of the previous ones never managed to escape the Solar System either. It would appear that humankind can only advance so far before the next Jupiter birth sends life crashing back to the dark ages, where the ten thousand or so survivors scattered around the Earth start again, and whichever tribe becomes eventually dominant dictates the language that becomes globally used. I wonder what the previous two dominant languages were."

"We'll never know. I suppose the only bright piece of science is that the gap between the Jupiter ejections maybe getting further apart. That might just be the bit of luck we need. But at some point in the future that luck might run out, and the next ejection may be a direct hit by a new celestial body crashing into the Earth. That really would be conclusive and final."

The pair stood opposite each other and reflected on what might or might not happen.

"Yep, probably a waste of time," they said in unison.

www.ingramcontent.com/pod-product-compliance
Lightning Source LLC
Chambersburg PA
CBHW040536170726

48295CB00012B/492